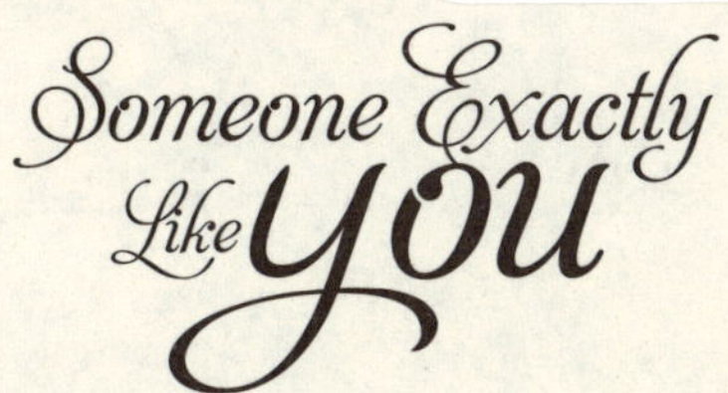

Esha Pandey is an author and an Indian Police Service (IPS) officer of the 2010 batch. Over the years, Esha has worked in various capacities and territories. In Delhi, Esha has served as Additional DCP in Central and North District, and as DCP Special Police Unit for Women and Children (SPUWAC). During her tenure, SPUWAC trained the highest number of girls in self-defence and established a Limca Record.

Before becoming a civil servant, she dabbled with the idea of being a journalist and worked with *The Times of India* as a copyeditor. She has also won a United Nations Future Policy Award for Excellence for the 'Best Short Story'. She made her debut as an author with her book *Kiss of Life and Other Stories,* a collection of short stories.

Her 'tall, dark and handsome' hero is her partner for life, her husband Rajiv, who supports her in all her endeavours. When she is not policing or writing, she is busy dealing with her two bundles of naughtiness, her sons.

She can be reached at twitter.com/PandeyEsha and https://www.facebook.com/EshaPandeyAuthor/

Someone Exactly Like You

ESHA PANDEY

RUPA

Published by
Rupa Publications India Pvt. Ltd 2019
7/16, Ansari Road, Daryaganj
New Delhi 110002

Sales centres:
Allahabad Bengaluru Chennai
Hyderabad Jaipur Kathmandu
Kolkata Mumbai

This is a work of fiction. Names, characters, places and incidents are either the product of the author's imagination or are used fictitiously and any resemblance to any actual person, living or dead, events or locales is entirely coincidental.

ISBN: 978-93-5333-362-1

First impression 2019

10 9 8 7 6 5 4 3 2 1

Printed at HT Media Ltd. Gr. Noida

For my sons Ayushmaan and Ishaan

1

'HAR ZULM KI *taufeeq hai zalim ki mohabbat, mazloom ke hisse me tasalli na dilasa,*' read the text from Yayu. Natasha smiled, put her phone back in her pocket and continued to walk towards her college. Yayu had been in love with her since school. He had declared his love for her innumerable times, but she had always laughed it off, saying, 'You are my best friend. Please don't complicate it.' It had been eight years since that first kiss on Valentine's Day, when he had asked her to be his date for a Valentine's party that his friends were hosting. She felt no sparks flying, no butterflies in her stomach when he kissed her. She told him as much the next day, and told him it would be better if they remain friends. He was heartbroken, but valiantly told her that he will always be there for her. Since then, he's been carrying a torch for her while she pretends she doesn't know about it. He sends her these messages, knowing her love for sher-o-shayari and ghazals, hoping to impress her, but she reads them for what they are and not what he wants to say.

Natasha was still repeating the couplet in her mind as she entered the red brick building of the School of Arts and Aesthetics. Today was the first day of the last semester of her degree course.

She was hurrying towards the school office when she heard Yayu call her and she turned around to see him walking towards her. He looked like a big ball of wool and fur; she wondered if he was wearing all the winter clothing he owned.

Yayu's grandfather was a history professor, who often interspersed history with mythology. His fascination with the epic, *Mahabharata,* and the history of the Pandavas and Kauravas had reflected in the names of all his children and grandchildren. Yayu's father's name was Nahush, and his paternal aunt was named Devyani. When he was born, it was divinely ordained—Yayu said, whenever he narrated the story of his birth—that he would be named Yayati, the son of Nahush, and conqueror of the world. 'Yayati' was shortened to 'Yayu' out of love, and it stuck.

'How many layers of clothing are you wearing?' she asked, a naughty smile on her face.

'Don't laugh, yaar,' he replied, sounding serious, 'you know I hate winters.'

'I know you do. You make it very apparent with your grunts and moans and constant complaining,' she said, hugging him and wishing him for New Year once again.

'Let's go to the canteen. I need some hot coffee in my system before I start the day,' he said, tugging at her bag and pointing her towards the canteen.

'No, let's get the folios first or it will be too crowded later.'

Folios were registration forms that had to be filled out every semester for re-registration. After collecting the folios, they headed to the canteen, while Natasha greeted everyone she met on her way. She loved the first day of the semester and the winter semester was her favourite. Jawaharlal Nehru University (JNU) looked very pretty in the winter months. There were flowers everywhere and the huge campus was lit up by the abundant sunshine. The numerous dhabas offered generous cups of hot, steaming coffee or tea, with masala Maggi for the depraved. It always gave her the feeling of a new beginning.

Huddled together in the crowded canteen, amidst tea mist and cigarette smoke, Yayu and Natasha were discussing the cinematic genius of Satyajit Ray. They were both specializing in cinematic studies and their hearts were filled with desire to be filmmakers in the future. The Apu Trilogy of Satyajit Ray had been their project for the winter vacations.

'His films are about the essence of the human race—relationships, emotions, struggles, conflicts, joys and sorrows,' said Natasha animatedly.

'I agree,' replied Yayu, 'his films demonstrate a deep understanding of human characters and situations. His depiction of the social and political milieu is pure genius.'

They continued discussing this film and that, till they realized that lunch was being served in the canteen and they had missed out on the registration for the day and would have to come back the next day.

'Now that we have successfully evaded registration and are free for the day, shall we catch a movie in Priya?' Yayu asked, referring to PVR Priya, which was close to JNU. Natasha and Yayu were regulars at the morning shows, as they were cheaper and student-friendly.

'No, not today,' said Natasha, taking her phone out of her pocket and dialling a number. With one hand covering the speaker, she said, 'I am meeting this hotshot artist today. He has a studio in Hauz Khas and…' she trailed off and started talking to someone on the phone. Yayu lit up another cigarette while waiting for her to finish the conversation, as they walked towards Ganga Dhaba to catch an auto.

'Done. I have to go to his studio today. I have been mailing him frequently since last month. He is going to have his big show in Paris this August and has consented to meet me. If I make a positive impression, he might also take me on as an intern…I know what you are thinking, but I feel by working with him and being in his circle, I might meet a few Bollywood biggies and embark on my journey as a director,' she said, making a little celebratory gesture with her hands in the air. 'You want to come to Hauz Khas with me?' she asked. 'We can have lunch and coffee later and I promise I won't lecture you when you check out the numerous firangs parading through the streets.'

He burst out laughing at her little catwalk. 'Oh please! None of the firangs match up to you,' he said with a lot of affection, 'but you carry on. I will catch up with others from the class. Let me know how the interview turns out and if I am going to lose you to Bollywood soon.' He signalled an auto and waved her goodbye as the auto pulled away.

∽

As her auto neared the artist's studio in Hauz Khas, Natasha took out her phone to look at the picture of her grandmother and seek her blessings. Orphaned at the innocent age of two years, Natasha had been raised by her grandmother, whom she lovingly called 'Nani'. Relatives from her father's side wanted to be rid of her as they didn't want to be reminded of the charmer, Natasha's mother, who wooed their son away and finally led to his unceremonious demise. It worked in favour of Nani, who wanted to hold on to any piece of her daughter that she could. Natasha's arrival gave her a new lease of life.

Natasha's mother, Sanyukta, had been a theatre actor and was known for her smokey eyes and beautiful smile. She had been a known flirt and had broken quite a few hearts before Natasha's father, Abhiyuday, said to her, 'Tread softly, as you tread on my dreams.' They were married within the week.

Parental approval was neither sought, nor given. Abhiyuday hailed from a conservative Brahmin family from Lucknow. His father, Shriram Shukla, had big dreams for his only son, who was born after the birth of three girls. His mother, Savitri, was a quintessential 'desi' mother. She wanted her son to be happy, but she was never able to raise her voice against the patriarch of the family. When Abhiyuday broke the news of his marriage to his parents, his mother fainted out of fear and his father became indifferent. They would have never approved of a Punjabi girl who worked in the theatre. Sanyukta's mother came around with the birth of Natasha, but Abhiyuday's parents never approved.

On the day of that fatal accident, Sanyukta and Abhiyuday had been riding in the back seat of the Maruti 800, which was being driven by their best friend, Shekhar. A bus had hit the car from behind and the impact was too much for all of them. Their bodies succumbed to the fatal injuries the following day. Natasha was oblivious to all this, cradled in the loving embrace of her Nani, who shook like a leaf with the shock of losing her only child.

Nani worked as a professor of psychology in JNU and lived close by, in Vasant Kunj. Natasha was sent to the best school in South Delhi and was encouraged to question everything. However, the line was drawn at any rules that Nani made—they could not be questioned. Study hours meant 'no games, only studies'. 'Lights out at nine' meant all shenanigans had to be finished by eight. Nani accepted nothing less than absolute commitment to learning. She was not after grades, but she wanted Natasha to be an informed individual, who could make her own decisions. Natasha grew up absorbing the rich culture of JNU. She started talking of Marx and Lenin as a tween, and was often taken to the plays at the Siri Fort and Kamani auditoriums. This infused in her a love for theatre, which later became a purpose. Her education in the Left was complete by the time she finished school. She was critiquing established norms and the written word so much that her Nani decided to send her to Miranda College in Delhi University to keep her away from JNU.

The 'Miranda years', as she referred to her time there, didn't fully keep her away from the culture of revolt and agitation. However, they successfully implanted in her a lust for fashion, and propelled her towards more hedonistic pursuits. She fell in love with Bollywood and masala movies. Her degree in English literature gave her ample opportunities to indulge in acting and directing plays in college. She realized that Bollywood movies were the easiest way to reach the masses. She started engaging with movies like *Ardh Satya, Satyakam* and *Bazaar,* which critiqued the society, and also movies like *Sholay, Deewar, Pakeezah* and *Bobby,* which were huge commercial successes. She wanted to pursue moviemaking because she realized it was an art, and also an industry that provided work to thousands of migrant workers from all over the country. The socialist in her wanted to contribute to the betterment of society in any way she could. It was this affair with theatre that made her apply for the course on cinematic studies in the first place. That Yayu was also applying for it, made her try harder to get in. She wanted to have a 'comrade' of her own to live through the ups and downs of the course, and who could be better than her best friend!

Walking through the bylanes of Hauz Khas, Natasha frequently checked her mobile for the GPS location of the address. The confident lady from the mobile said, 'Turn right and walk 200 metres'; she did as instructed. The lady said, 'You have reached your destination'. She was standing right in front of 'Mir', the studio of artist Gazaffar Mir. He was best known for his cinematic genius in depicting the life of a courtesan in Lucknow during the pre-independence era, through a multi-starrer blockbuster movie in the 1980s. Since then, he had indulged in painting and couture. His paintings had graced galleries all over the world and he was due to have his first show of paintings, inspired by the Hindi movie industry—or Bollywood—in Paris.

Natasha was taken directly to Gazaffar, who made her comfortable and asked her to call him by his given name.

'So, why do you want to intern for me?' asked Gazaffar.

'I want to learn from you,' she said seriously. 'I have been studying about your work, and your love for movies as a medium of expression has inspired me.'

'But you have applied to be an intern for my painting exhibition,' he cut in, 'and not as an assistant director for my movie.'

'Yes,' she said, trying not to be rattled by him. 'I want to be associated with you in any which way,' she said, smiling a little. 'You are an institution. I can learn so much just by being around you. Please give me this opportunity.'

Natasha knew what her plan was, but she didn't need to tell him that. She needed some time to be on her own near the artist to soak up the nitty-gritties of art, before she felt confident enough to apply to be his assistant director (AD). *A girl's gotta do what a girl's gotta do.*

His face softened a bit as his eyes shone from the smile lurking behind. 'You are hired,' he said, getting up from his comfortable chair. 'My secretary will give you the details.'

2

NATASHA WAS HUMMING an old ghazal from the Hindi movie *Arth*, *'Tum itna jo muskura rahe ho, kya gham hai jisko chhupa rahe ho,'* as the picturesque hills of Uttarakhand flashed past her window. She was travelling on the bus from Dehradun to Mussoorie. The last few months had just rolled by and her internship with Gazaffar Mir was to begin in two days. Her Nani had been very apprehensive about sending her to Mussoorie for the internship with an 'artist type', whom she didn't trust at all, but had to bow in front of Natasha's reason and unrelenting will. Nani had offered to go with her and settle her in Landour, a township close to Mussoorie, where Gazaffar Mir stayed, but Natasha refused point-blank.

'I can manage on my own. Why are you being paranoid, Nani? Mama was travelling the whole world with her theatre group at my age. You never had a problem with that,' she threw her hands up in the air in frustration, 'then why now?'

'I am not being paranoid. Don't brand me "crazy". Circumstances have changed, society has changed. I am all for smart, independent women; it's just that I fear for you...but don't worry,' she said, putting a couple of books in one of the bags that were strewn across her room. 'I am not going to stop you. I trust you and believe you are completely capable of taking care of yourself.'

'Yes, Nani. I am,' she said, as Nani came forward and hugged her.

While Nani was a hard nut to crack, Yayu was even harder. He just wouldn't hear her point of view. She didn't like that Yayu was behaving like her boyfriend or that he even thought he had any authority to stop her from following her heart, but she knew he meant well. He was still in love with her; she wanted him to meet someone new and fall in love. For that to happen, she needed to be away from him. 'How can I convince you if you just shut me out?' Natasha asked.

'There is nothing to talk about. I am really happy for you, Natasha. I just want to come with you so I can see if you are safe,' he said in anger.

'Yayu, don't be like that. You have known for four months now. I have to go; I *want* to go. It will be very good for my career and my growth as an artist. I finally have Nani on my side and I need you to understand as well,' she said, holding his hand.

But Yayu didn't come around. He came to pick her up in his car the day of her journey to Dehradun. Once she was settled in her berth and the train whistled, Yayu hugged her and left. She received a message one hour later: '*ye na thi hamari kismet ki visal-e-yar hota, agar aur jite rehte yahi intezar hota*'. He had put a winking smiley at the end of the message, to soften the blow. Yayu was very dramatic and even when he knew that Natasha was coming back in a month's time, he was behaving as if she had left him forever. She was still thinking about what to say in her reply when the tiredness of the whole day caught up with her and the steady motion of the train lulled her to sleep.

As they pulled into Dehradun Railway Station, she awoke, got off the train and headed towards the Information Desk. She was told that the bus for Mussoorie was ready to leave and it would reach Library Point in an hour, from where she could take a taxi to Landour. Since it was only 7 in the morning, she would reach her destination latest by 10. She did exactly what the polite lady at the Desk had told her, and was about to reach Library Point in ten minutes, the conductor informed her.

Her transition from the bus to the taxi was swift and hassle-free. The taxi drivers were used to handling tourists and were very polite. However, the weather was beginning to play up. It was drizzling by the time they started for Landour. She had given the address to the driver and was checking on Google Maps if he was taking the correct route. The rain slowed down the journey and it took her an hour to reach her destination. Natasha always had trouble travelling in the hills. She had vertigo, and the narrow, meandering roads of the hills made her nauseous. To keep it down, she generally avoided eating while travelling. In fact, she had not eaten anything because she had decided to eat at Landour.

By the time she reached the address given by Gazaffar's secretary, it was raining very heavily. The house was a huge old British-era bungalow with a big portico, situated on the top of a hill. The taxi went right through the main entrance, the gate to which was promptly opened by the old guard. The taxi driver took out Natasha's bags and kept them on the stairs leading to the front door. She was busy scanning the place when she heard the old guard call out to her. She couldn't hear what he said as the distance between the gate and the portico was enough for the rain to drown out his voice. She asked the driver if he had heard what the guard said, but he just asked for the payment of his fare. She handed him a ₹500 note and he left without another word.

The guard waved frantically at her as the taxi swept past him, 'What is it?' she asked. He was walking towards her now. He was a frail old man from the mountains. Age had slowed him down; she could see that he was walking with a lot of difficulty, with a stick in one hand and the umbrella, protecting him from the heavy downpour, in the other. She figured that he lived in the guard room next to the gate, from the few clothes that had been left to dry on the lines, but were now soaking wet because of the unexpected rains.

By the time the guard joined her, she had had a look at the front door, which was locked. She could see that all the doors and windows were shut. There was nobody else there. Her heart was thumping with fear and excitement when the old man said, 'Beta, nobody is here. Who are you?'

'What do you mean "nobody's here"? I am Natasha Kapoor. I start my internship with Gazaffar Mir today. I was given this address by his secretary, Neeta!' she replied frantically.

'Oh, alright. Neeta had called to tell me that Gazaffar Sahab won't be coming here after all. His son met with an accident, so he had to go be with him. Did she not inform you?' he asked matter-of-factly.

'No, she didn't inform me. What am I supposed to do now?' she was talking to herself, trying to dial Neeta's number on the phone. Finally, she got through.

'Hi, Neeta, this is Natasha. I just reached Landour. This guard is telling me that Gazaffar Sir is not coming here?'

To this, Neeta replied with a customary apology and her 'How could I be so forgetful' drill and offered to reimburse whatever she had spent on the journey back and forth.

Nothing could be done. She was angry and extremely

disappointed that Gazaffar had cancelled her internship. She had told the whole world about it and also fought with her best friend. Her Nani would be so worried if she knew what had happened. She couldn't let them know, so she just messaged both her and Yayu that she was alright and would contact them once she had more time.

Then she sat down on the cot offered by the guard, who had also made a cup of tea for her. He informed her that she should start walking back if she wanted to make it to Mussoorie before evening. But the rain was not stopping and she had two trolley bags and a backpack to handle. She asked the guard if she could buy his raincoat, to which he replied, 'I don't sell things. You can take it, beta. You are just like my granddaughter. I wish I could do more.'

The raincoat was big for her and ensured that she was fully covered. Her bags, however, were a different story altogether. She had been walking down the hill for about two hours when she heard the horn of a vehicle approaching her from behind. She stopped and started signalling the driver to stop.

It was a truck, which pulled up next to her. A hairy Sardarji peered out of the driver's window and asked in a heavy Punjabi accent, 'What happened? Where do you want to go? I am going to Mussoorie,' as his helper stared at her from behind him.

Natasha regretted stopping the truck the moment she set her eyes on the hairy driver and the lecherous helper. She refused to get into it.

'No, thank you. I am sorry I stopped you. I will walk; my house is very close by,' she lied, feeling nervous as the helper joined her on the road.

The driver became more insistent and the helper tried to take control of her bags, 'What will you do in this rain? Come, we will drop you to your home.'

It had become pitch dark by now and it was only five in the evening.

'Nahi, Sardarji, I don't want to go. Please carry on,' she refused firmly and tried to walk ahead.

It had become quite dark by this time because of the continuous rain. Her heart was thumping with fear as the driver-helper duo pestered her. She started walking fast, dragging her bags behind her. The helper was still following her, while the driver drove the truck at a slow pace next to Natasha, all the time talking to her from the window, 'Arre madam, come, we will drop you,' he insisted, signalling his helper to take her bags.

When the helper tried to get fresh with her, she left her bags and ran for her life. She ran faster than she had ever imagined she could, with the helper chasing her and the driver following in the truck. The long day started to catch up with her. She had not had anything to eat, and the stress of the 'non-existent internship' and now these terrifying men just added to her misery. As her legs gave way, she all but gave up hope. At the exact moment that the helper caught up with her, she saw a car approaching from the opposite side. She screamed for help and signalled with flailing arms. The car stopped with a screech next to the truck. She screamed, 'Please help me. Please help...' as the helper put his hand on her mouth.

As the driver of the car emerged, the truck driver signalled the helper to leave the girl and get back in the truck, and they sped off with lightning speed.

The car driver came running towards her, just in time to catch her as she collapsed from exhaustion.

3

NATASHA CAME TO, as the stranger was setting her down in the passenger seat of the car. The moment she realized what was happening, she started screaming and squirming to get out of the car.

'No, no, let me go,' she shouted.

'Hey, calm down,' he said, trying to pacify her. 'You are safe. Calm down,' he repeated. 'I am just trying to help you. You are safe with me,' he said as she looked at him with fear and doubt in her eyes.

His calming words and helpful demeanour soothed her a bit.

'Why don't you open the top buttons of your raincoat? You will be more comfortable,' he suggested and her hand automatically went to the buttons. She saw her backpack kept near her feet. *He must have taken it off my shoulder,* she thought.

She couldn't see him clearly, but his husky voice and kind eyes made her feel comfortable. As he crossed in front of the car to join her at the driver's seat, she got a good look at him. He was tall, around six feet, dressed in formals, had a confident stride and sported a crew cut. His car and his clothes confirmed that he was well-off. His diction certified good education.

'What are you doing here in this weather?' he asked as he sat down in the driver's seat.

'It's a long story,' she replied.

When he realized that she was not going to volunteer any more information, he took out a bottle of water from the glove compartment and offered it to her.

'Have some water. Don't worry, you are safe with me,' he said again, urging her to have a sip.

She took the offered bottle and gulped down its contents.

'So, where are you going?' he asked again. The light inside the car highlighted his dark hair and kind eyes. He reminded her of someone but she couldn't place him.

She kept the empty bottle in the bottle compartment of the door and replied, 'I am going back to Mussoorie.'

'What are you doing here? Who are you? You have to give me some details if you want my help,' he insisted.

'Okay, I will if you just keep driving up the hill. I have left my bags somewhere by the road. If we hurry up, we may find them,' she appealed.

He complied, and the headlights of the car lit up the road and the heavy downpour.

'My name is Natasha,' she began, 'I was here to start an internship with the artist Gazaffar Mir, who lives in Landour. Unfortunately, his son met with an accident and his secretary failed to inform me. So, when I landed here, I had nowhere to go and it started raining cats and dogs. Since then, I have been walking with my bags, trying to get to Dehradun via Mussoorie. I stopped that truck before I realized who was in it. These people wanted to hurt me, so I started running. But, thankfully, before they could harm me, you showed up.' And then abruptly, she added, 'Stop.

There—those are my bags.' He got out of the car and collected the bags and kept them securely in the boot of the car.

'Can you please drop me to the nearest bus station?' she requested as he started driving again.

'Look, Miss Natasha, the weather is very bad and you are in the hills. Even if I drop you to the station, there is no guarantee that you would find a bus for Dehradun in this weather. I would suggest that you come to my home, which is nearby, rest for the night and plan the next course of action in the morning,' he said gently. When he saw the shadow of doubt descend upon her, he added, 'My grandmother and my housekeeper stay with me, so you will be very comfortable.'

That did comfort her, but this guy had still not introduced himself, so she asked, 'What is your name?'

'Veer,' he replied. It was still raining heavily so she didn't disturb him while he navigated the hilly road. She kept checking for network on her phone but she had no luck with it. She was thinking about how worried her Nani might be if she knew what all was happening to her. Yayu must have tried her number umpteen times as well. She must call both of them the moment they reach his home, she decided. They had still not travelled much when the exhaustion of the day caught up with her and she fell asleep.

She woke up with a start at the sound of the horn. It took her a few seconds to come back to her senses. By the time she realized where she was, a guard opened a big iron gate and they entered a driveway. The gravel made a crushing noise beneath the tyres of the car. And within a few seconds, they were parked beneath a big porch. It was very dark and there was no electricity. She could just make out that it was a fairly big house.

A middle-aged lady came out with an emergency light and

said, 'Sir, where have you been? The electricity has been gone for an hour now and we have been very worried about you. They are talking about a cloudburst on the radio.' She went quiet when she saw Natasha.

'Lydia, please help Miss Natasha out of the car while I grab her bags,' he said, coming out of the driver's seat.

Lydia rushed to her side and tried to help her out. Natasha was burning up with fever. She wobbled out of the car and flopped to the ground with a loud thud, oblivious to her surroundings.

4

RUMBLING THUNDER WOKE her up with a start. *Where was she?* It was still a little dark outside. She reached for her phone to check the time. It was fifteen past ten in the morning and she was still in bed. *Whose bed? Whose room was this?* She tried to place herself mentally and relaxed a bit when she remembered that she had been saved by a stranger. *Thank God for him, I am okay,* she thought as she looked around the cozy room. The light from the dying embers in the fireplace gave the small room an orange hue. It was done up in a bohemian style with vibrant colours. Three walls were painted chrome yellow and the fourth wall, the signature wall behind the fireplace, in orange. The mantel above the fireplace was home to lots of photos in frames, which she couldn't see clearly from where she lay. The bed was made of wrought iron and was covered with a bright and colourful handmade quilt. A chair in the corner of the room, next to a French window, looked very inviting and she got up to look out of the window.

The curtains were cream and orange, and made of very fine cotton. She parted them to peep outside. The view was mind-blowing. She was in a mansion. Everything was covered in white snow till the eyes could see. She was immediately filled with happiness. She had never experienced snow and this would be her first time. The very next moment, she thought of calling Yayu and Nani. But there was no network on her phone. She panicked a little as she realized that if the phone network was down, the transportation network might also be down. She located the small door to the bathroom and got dressed in a jiffy.

She picked up both her bags kept near the bathroom door and her backpack from the table next to the bed. She opened the door of the room to find herself in a gallery that was beautifully lit up and leading to a very spacious sitting area. Big, comfortable white sofas with colourful throws and pillows yet again emphasized the bohemian style of the room. A bigger fireplace kept the room warm, while the view of the mountains from the huge windows on the other side of the room took her breath away. There was no one in sight, so she kept her bags on the side and proceeded to absorb the scenic beauty.

Last night's happenings were sketchy in her mind. She remembered a maid called Lydia trying to help her out of the car. She remembered fainting outside the car and then recalled someone feeding her some soup and giving her some medicine, while she slipped in and out of delirium. She remembered Veer carrying her down the corridor to the room and tucking her in the bed. And then nothing! She was still thinking about all that had happened since she had left her home, when she heard footsteps.

'Good morning,' said Veer, as she turned. He was wearing black track pants, a big bulky hand-knitted sweater and had casually draped a shawl around his shoulders. He looked majestic in his surroundings. Natasha again felt that she had seen him somewhere, but couldn't place him.

'Good morning,' she replied sheepishly. 'Sorry for being such a problem last night. I don't know what came upon me. I don't faint like that, ever.'

'No, no. Don't apologize. You weren't a problem at all,' he replied, and then asked with concern, 'How are you feeling now? You had very high fever last night. We gave you the medicine that was available and Lydia was with you till you fell asleep. Hope you are better now. Have you had any breakfast?' On her refusal, he called out to Lydia to bring in the tray that had been laid out for Natasha.

'Dadi and I had breakfast sometime back. We didn't want to disturb you, so didn't wake you up,' he explained. 'Dadi is in her room. I will take you to meet her once you have had breakfast.'

She was trying very hard to concentrate on what he was saying as her mind raced to identify him. She knew she had seen him somewhere, but did not know where. She was still contemplating asking him when Lydia walked in with her breakfast. The smell of steaming hot coffee and buttered toast made her forget everything else and she devoured the meal.

When she had satiated her appetite, she asked him, 'When can I leave? The weather is getting worse and it would be best if I leave immediately. Do you know when the next bus for Dehradun will leave?'

'I called the bus station before you got up. It seems all buses have been cancelled as the road to Dehradun is blocked due to landslides. In fact, there is no electricity, we are using generators and the telephone network is down as well. There is no way you can leave today or in the next few days,' he said, leaving her shocked.

'How is that possible? There must be a way out of here. I will walk the whole way, but I need to get out of here,' she said dramatically. 'I need to contact my grandmother. She must be going crazy with worry.'

He looked helpless.

'As you can see, it's still snowing. Even with chains on the tyres, the vehicles will find it very difficult to navigate and then there are landslides that take days to clear. So, as far as leaving today is concerned, you can't really do it,' he said matter-of-factly. 'However,' he continued, 'I have a satellite phone in my study. You can use that to call your grandmother.'

That pacified her a bit, but she still insisted on making the call as soon as possible. Veer led her to a room at the far end of the house. It was tastefully done in leather and wood and had a very manly appeal. She didn't have enough time to admire it as he handed her the receiver and said, 'Dial the number,' and left the room.

Nani had been more worried than Natasha had anticipated. She was literally on the verge of tears as she heard Natasha's voice. Natasha told her many times that she was alright and would try to contact her as often as possible, given the circumstances. She asked her to contact Yayu also and tell him that she was safe. With much difficulty, she convinced Nani that she was well and would be home when the weather becomes better.

As she put the receiver down, she saw the large showcase full of trophies. At least two of them looked like Filmfare trophies. She went to take a closer look at them. They were *indeed* Filmfare trophies awarded to the Best Director. Her heart started beating faster as it dawned on her why Veer looked familiar. The big, laminated poster of *Khoya Khoya Chand*, featuring Amyra Singh and Rajyavardhan, and directed by Veer Singh Tomar, confirmed her suspicion. Her heart stopped for a second as Veer entered the room.

It started beating again when he said, 'So, now you know who I am and you are scared to be alone with me. Don't worry, I won't harm you,' and quickly left the room.

Natasha was left gasping for breath as she came to terms with the fact that she had spent the last night and this morning in the company of the devilishly handsome, bad boy of the cine world, Veer Singh Tomar. She remembered reading something about his messy divorce proceedings and accusations of sexual and mental abuse and domestic violence by his wife, Amyra Singh. She had read about his violent streak on sets with his wife. She remembered reading a whole issue of a leading women's magazine, on domestic abuse, with Veer on its cover page. Film magazines also readily carried snippets of his tantrums on set and how people tolerated it because he was a very talented filmmaker. She liked his 'bad boy' image, but the reports of his anger in the workspace made her sceptical. Incidentally, Amyra had never come out in the open to defend Veer and refute any of the stories. To her credit, she had never confirmed the accusations made against Veer by the media, but her complaint to the police had gone viral and that was the confirmation everyone was looking for. As she followed Veer out of the room, she realized that she was not at all disappointed at being held up in the palatial bungalow with this handsome stranger.

In fact, she was looking forward to making the most of it.

5

FOR THE LAST few hours, she had been sitting alone in the guest room allotted to her. She had tried to keep herself busy, watching episodes of *Big Bang Theory* on her laptop but it didn't really help. Her thoughts kept going to the handsome stranger whom she had been crushing on since time immemorial. Natasha was bubbling with excitement and wanted to tell someone about this. She tried her phone many times but there was no network. Finally, she gave up and decided to watch the sitcom but it was pointless. All she could think about was Veer. She couldn't believe her luck. In the past few hours, she had made up her mind to make the most of her situation and make up for the lost opportunity in terms of the internship. *If not Gazaffar Mir, she could learn the tricks of the trade from the bad boy of Bollywood,* she thought, with a twinkle in her eyes and a mysterious smile on her lips. *But where was the bad boy hiding?* she thought to herself as she left the room to search for him.

The house was huge, with many rooms and galleries connecting them. In the middle of the house was a big sitting area with huge French windows. Two galleries led from either side of the room to different sections of the house. While she was housed in the guest area of the house, the opposite gallery led to the owner's part of the house, as she had gathered from Lydia. She was walking softly as she entered the owner's portion of the house. The corridor was lit with warm light and many beautiful family photos were hanging on the wall. She was mesmerized by the happy boy in the pictures. It was Veer, she was sure of it. He had the same glint in his eyes and the same smile lurking on his lips. She didn't realize when she had come to the end of the corridor and near the gym. She heard the heavy, laboured breathing of someone as she opened the door. She was not prepared for what she saw.

It was an onslaught on all her senses, all at once. Veer was on the bench press, lifting weights. He was wearing only his track pants, shoes and a black sweatband on his forehead. Natasha stopped dead in her tracks. The flexed muscles of his arms and the tiny droplets of sweat on his upper lip made her heart skip a beat. She watched as he lifted and made a guttural sound. She had never seen a half-naked man, with such an awesome body, at such close quarters. It ignited feelings in her she did not know existed.

She must have made some involuntary gesture that made Veer look her way. She felt a blush creep on to her cheeks, as he put the weight down, wrapped a towel around himself and walked towards her.

'How long have you been standing there?' he asked, taking a sip from his bottle. Natasha felt her throat become parched as one drop of water escaped his lips and travelled down his perfect Adam's apple towards his belly button and lower still; she dared not look.

'I just entered the room,' she lied. 'I have been looking for you for some time now; you just vanished,' she said, trying to sound as normal as possible, even though her heart was racing at the speed of an engine and she was sure the thudding sound was loud enough for him to hear.

'I have been hiding from you,' he said with a naughty smile, and she felt butterflies in her stomach. 'There, have I made you uncomfortable?' he laughed. 'I was with Dadi and then I came for a workout. Did you want something?'

She didn't know how to reply. She knew exactly what she wanted, but could she ask him for that? She would love to be his apprentice, but how would he take it? Still, she decided to broach the topic and ventured, 'Actually, there is something...I wonder if you would be willing to help me.'

'Go ahead,' he reassured her.

'As you know I was here to intern with the artist Gazaffar Mir. That did not materialize because of his son's accident. What you don't know is that I am a student of Cinema Studies in JNU, your alma mater. I am a big fan of your work and it would be absolutely awesome if you could let me help you on your current project, even if it involves fetching tea for you while you work. Please don't judge me; I couldn't have let go of this opportunity without asking you. I would have regretted it for the rest of my life. I had to ask,' she said, looking at him with a mixed expression of hope and guilt.

She felt embarrassed about taking advantage of him—he had rescued her, had given her refuge in his home and, now, she was asking more of him. She felt she had cornered him. But he was known to be ruthless and if the stories were to be believed, he would not have any trouble saying 'no' to her if he wanted to.

He looked at her deeply, as if searching inside her soul, and then looked away. He pulled on his T-shirt and a sweatshirt, put his towel around his neck and walked away from her. She was left wondering, when he opened the door to another room and vanished. She felt stupid to have made a complete fool of herself. The walk back to her room was a walk of shame and disappointment. Maybe she should have waited and asked him at a more appropriate time. In her eagerness, she forgot how senior he was and how badly it must have reflected on her character, taking advantage of a man who had been so nice to her. She felt a gloom descend upon her like a thick blanket of snow, not to be easily shaken off.

6

SHE WAS SITTING in the lovely chair facing the beautiful French window, lost in thought. She had been brazen enough to ask Veer for an internship. The fact that he didn't reply immediately, and didn't even make any attempt to reply the following day, had embarrassed her deeply. She was wondering how she was ever going to face him, when Lydia brought in a steaming cup of coffee and some madeleines. The smell of coffee made her realize how hungry she was. The madeleines were as light as the snow outside and she gobbled them up quickly.

With the cup of coffee in her hands, she was looking at the horizon, when she noticed Veer walking towards the portico. He was dressed casually in a big North Face jacket with its hood up, jeans and snow boots. He had a leather glove on one hand and was pulling on the other one, when something made him look up. Her hand waved an involuntarily hello and he waved back. He made a gesture, asking her to come down. She double-checked, asking in return if he meant to call her down. He nodded. She put down her cup and bolted down the stairs. He had walked inside and was standing at the portico to receive her.

'Lydia has laid out a jacket and boots for you. They belong

to my cousin, who visits here often to meet Dadi. Please wear them if you want to be comfortable walking in the snow,' he said, directing her to a receiving room where the jacket and the shoes were laid out.

'Are we going for a walk?' she asked, pulling on the boots.

'Well I was, and then I saw you standing at the window, looking forlorn and I took pity on you,' he said with such panache that she felt ashamed to her roots.

'Oh, you don't have to take me with you. Please go ahead. I am perfectly fine,' she replied, trying to pull off the boot.

He laughed and said, 'Oh come on, I was only joking. Let me show you around.'

She quickly wore the jacket and they started walking. The moment they were out of the house, he took out a pack of cigarettes and sought her permission to smoke. There was nothing sexy about smoking. Yayu smoked and she too had tried it in college but never got hooked. But the way Veer kept the cigarette on the tip of his lower lip and leaned in to light it, set her heart racing. She couldn't take her eyes off him as he dragged the smoke deep inside him.

'Dadi doesn't like me smoking and I can't seem to let go of it,' he said with a tinge of guilt in his voice.

She didn't want to add to his misery by saying it is injurious to health; he knew what he was doing. He walked fast and she was having difficulty keeping pace with him. Snow covered the ground for as far as she could see. She was thinking of all the Yash Chopra movies and their signature songs in the hills. She could definitely sympathize with the heroine now. It was extremely cold and she wondered how they would shoot in a sari and blouse; just the thought of that sent a shiver down her spine. Veer noticed that she was lost in her thoughts.

'Penny for your thoughts.'

She looked up. 'Nothing much. This is my first experience with snow. I am thinking of all the Yash Chopra heroines and what they must have endured. I mean, it sure looks romantic but it is so cold,' she said with a worried expression on her face.

Veer was smiling now. 'So, this is your first time seeing snow. How would you capture the beauty of this moment on camera?'

His question surprised her. *Was he giving her a chance to prove herself?* she thought for a moment and then said, 'I will keep it real. I will begin with the snowflakes and how they melt when they touch the warmth of the skin and leave a little drop of water behind. I will show how the lack of proper clothing for a cold weather like this makes a warring couple hold hands and cuddle. The man would be towering over the woman and trying to protect her from the cold wind and she would hug him tight to share with him the heat from her body. The snowflakes will get caught in their hair and one would fall on her lips. He would try to kiss that flake away but she wouldn't let him go and would become more insistent as their tongues found each other.'

'Cut,' he said out loud. 'This is Bollywood, Madam. Where are you going?'

'I was just going to add that then the man would break the kiss and pull the woman towards a Jeep parked nearby and they would head back with a promise to continue at home. Keeping it real,' she said with a wink.

'I like your spunk,' he said. 'I have given your proposal some thought and would be willing to take you on, if you are still interested.'

Her heart stopped beating; her stomach turned inside out. 'Do you mean it?'

She had stopped walking and he had walked a few steps ahead.

'Yes, I mean it,' he said with a smile.

She jumped with joy. 'Thank you so much. You won't regret it. You have no idea what this means to me.'

'I think I do,' he replied, clearly amused, and lit up another cigarette, as they turned to walk back to the house.

The light from the lighter lit up his features. His hair flopped over his brows, giving him a roguish look. His proud nose and kind eyes gave his face roughness and warmth at the same time. He was so handsome that her whole body reacted to him. She felt drawn towards him and wondered for a moment if it was a good idea to work with him at such close quarters.

7

DINNER WAS A quick affair and she finally got to see Dadi at the dinner table. Dadi was nothing like she had imagined. She was full of life, even though she had to rely on a wheelchair and a nurse. After dinner, they gathered around the fireplace in the big living room, with coffee to serve as a nightcap. Dadi asked Natasha about her family and how she ended up here. Natasha narrated the story of her life animatedly to Dadi, oblivious to Veer's reactions to her narrative. Dadi was concerned about her safe return and her stay at the house, and ordered Veer to take care of both.

'You are such a lovely girl,' said Dadi, looking at her. 'We must take care of you while you stay here with us. Veer, please make sure that her stay here is comfortable. I mean, as comfortable as possible in this weather. She should be able to contact anyone she wants on the satellite phone and keep a lookout for vehicular traffic. She should be able to leave as soon as buses start plying.'

'Dadi, don't worry, I will take care of her and pack her off as soon as possible,' Veer said with a wink. His smile was infectious. She was completely bowled over by his looks and his kind manners. But then there was this rumoured dark side, which allegedly made him very moody and quiet and that scared her. As Dadi bid them farewell for the night, Natasha also got ready to retire. But Veer had something else planned.

'We must discuss the terms of your internship if you want to start work immediately,' he looked at her with amusement, as she stopped mid-air while getting up from the sofa.

'Yes, we should,' she said, sitting down again.

It was still snowing outside and the snow was pilling up. She was sure that her stay here would be longer than anyone could hope, and it would be best to make the most of this time.

'What do you want me to do?'

'Would you like to have some brandy?' he asked, making a peg for himself.

She didn't want to, but couldn't be rude, so she agreed. He handed her the glass and sat down on the sofa across from her, near the fireplace. He nudged the dying embers in the fireplace and added some more wood from the sack kept next to him. It lit up again with an orangish-yellowish hue. The light from the fire caught his glass and it looked like he was drinking liquid gold. She was focusing on his glass when his fingers caught her attention. He was still wearing his wedding ring. He did not, even once, talk about his wife and the messy divorce proceedings they were caught in. She had read that he had never retaliated against his wife in public. *Was he still in love with her?* she wondered.

'I am currently working on a new film and would be willing to take you on as an AD. Your internship would begin today—I mean tonight. You have to help me with the research for the script, help me organize my stuff, search locations—anything and everything I need. You will have to work 24x7 and at the end of the week, I will decide if you are fit to be my AD. Is that okay?' he asked, looking intently at her.

'Yes,' she said, without a second thought. 'I am willing to work as hard as needed,' she added with determination, wondering if she had said it too quickly.

He got up to make another peg.

'Would you have some more?' he asked her.

'No, I think I will call it a night. I'm feeling quite tired.'

He nodded in agreement. 'Just one more thing. If you have any questions about my wife or my life, please ask me right now. I don't want you snooping around. Let us get it over with. I know you are dying of curiosity. So, please just ask what you need to know, so we can move ahead.'

She was caught unawares by his dispassionate—almost disgusted—attitude towards her interest. She thought it was unfair that she should be judged when he was the one who had made a spectacle of himself—and he lived his life in public view! But she couldn't let go of this golden opportunity to question him.

'Do you still love her?' she asked in all sincerity.

She saw anger in his eyes and darkness lurking within them, as he absorbed the magnanimity of her question. He looked away from her and downed the contents of the glass. She thought she must say something to break the silence.

'I asked because you are still wearing your wedding ring.'

That made him look at his ring. He got up to make another peg for himself and leaned against the corner of the fireplace, looking at her as he answered, 'I wear it out of habit. I don't know if I still love her… Anything else?'

She thought about asking him about the accusations of domestic violence and abuse made by her, but she didn't want to anger him, so she tactfully asked if the stories published in the media were true.

He looked at her directly and replied, 'Most of them are true.' She felt a little uncomfortable that he didn't deny anything. *Was she safe working with someone who had a history of domestic violence and abuse?* Her anxiety must have been visible on her face because he said, 'Yes, you should be scared of working with me. Any more questions?'

'What is your current status—I mean, are you divorced or separated?' she asked seriously.

'Why? Are you interested?' he asked with a naughty smile on his face and a twinkle in his eyes.

She blushed to her toes. 'No, I am not. Remember, *you* permitted me to ask you anything,' she retorted quickly.

'Since you are not interested, I choose not to answer this question. If, by any chance, you become interested, ask me again,' he quipped with a smile. 'And now, we should call it a night.' He got up and left without a second look at her.

Natasha was left stranded in the middle of the big room, wondering if she *was* interested.

8

SOMETIME DURING THE middle of the night, the central heating gave way and the bitter cold from the outside started creeping in. Natasha slept fitfully through the night, mostly dreaming of Veer. She was being held up at gunpoint and he came to her rescue; she was walking hand in hand with him and he stopped to brush away a snowflake that had fallen on her nose. In all the situations, she was romantically involved with Veer and when she woke up, her heart was beating faster and she was very uncomfortable; so much so that, even in an extremely cold room, she came out from under the quilt and ran to the bathroom to splash water on her face.

She was still in the bathroom when she heard a knock on the door. It was Lydia. She had brought a cup of tea with some biscuits. She told Natasha that the central heating had stopped because there was something wrong with one of the generators. Now, they could get central heating only after that was fixed. Natasha asked her if the lamps in the rooms would be lit. Lydia replied in the affirmative and said that they would have to use fuel efficiently as the weather had worsened and there was no hope of its clearing up soon.

'How will Dadi manage without the central heating?' she

asked Lydia, concerned about the old lady.

'In Dadi's room, we have kept an oil heater. That regulates the room temperature just as well as central heating does. Though she *was* complaining about the increased pain in her knees,' Lydia replied. 'Should I bring your breakfast here or would you like to join the others in the dining room?'

'I will come down for breakfast. When will you serve?'

With one hour to go before breakfast would be served, Natasha decided to take a walk. She was looking like an eskimo, all covered from head to toe. Navigating through the snow-laden road, she came to a point from where she could see the snow-covered peaks of the mighty Himalayas. The beauty of the scene overwhelmed her and somehow made her miss Nani and Yayu. They would be so worried about her. Yayu would definitely scream at her for not calling more often, but what could she do under these circumstances. There was no electricity or telephone connection, the satellite phone that Veer had was very expensive and she didn't want to ask him to use it repeatedly. She was already imposing so much on him.

On her way back, she thought about her internship and how lucky she was. If everything worked out as she hoped, she might end up working as Veer's AD. That would be an awesome break. She would have to work very hard and agree to all his whims and fancies. She was absolutely determined by the time she reached the breakfast table and found him frowning at Lydia.

'Please tell her that I am indisposed next time she calls. I don't want to talk to her,' Veer reprimanded.

Lydia sheepishly replied, 'Yes, Sir. I am sorry, it won't happen again.'

Natasha didn't know if she should stay or leave. Veer ended

her confusion and called her in to have breakfast. Dadi also joined them later and the phone call was forgotten as the discussion meandered from Delhi to Nehru to silk saris and, finally, to movies. Veer apprised Dadi of the new understanding between Natasha and himself—that she will be working as an intern with him and if he likes her working style, he might take her on as an AD for his next film.

'You are lucky, Natasha. Veer is very good at what he does and works very hard on his films. You will learn a lot from him. But be ready to be scolded from time to time,' Dadi said with a smile.

'Yes, Dadi,' Natasha replied and poured another cup of tea for herself. On a cold morning like this, the comfort of buttered toast, cutlets and tea had soothed her soul and she was longing to be in the comfort of her room, to lie under the orange quilt and go back to dreaming.

But that was not to be. Veer said he would try to fix the central heating, working on the generator kept at the back of the house.

Dadi encouragingly said, 'Natasha will accompany you, won't you, Natasha? You can show her my pomegranate tree while you are there. I planted that tree when Veer was a young boy. If I could, I would have walked with you to that tree.'

Natasha was put on the spot and had to agree.

Veer looked reluctant but said, 'Alright. You can come with me.' Natasha quickly finished her tea and got up to leave as Veer started moving. She followed him to the back of the house, which was like a big garage. It housed the mains for the plumbing, the electric connections and the heating for the building. There were two big generators, one of which was working. Veer directly went to the quiet one. He checked the alternator and the fuel system and found them to be working. Then he looked at the voltage regulator and found the rotor to be at fault. It would have to be changed, Veer said.

Natasha leaned in to see what he was pointing at. She was too close to him. He was explaining to her that the rotor converts the DC voltage to AC voltage and helps in the regulation of the voltage, but all Natasha could hear was the loud beating of her heart as his manly smell—a mixture of musk and Old Spice cologne—played havoc with her senses. She was trying to concentrate very hard on what he was saying but all she could think about were his large shoulders and broad back. He pointed at something and she had to lean in further to see. She tripped on the toolbox kept on the floor and he caught her just in time. She landed right in his arms.

She felt an electric wave pass through her body. She was so attracted to him that, for a few seconds there, she couldn't reason. Her heart was hammering against her ribcage. Her breasts were tingling. Her stomach was doing summersaults. She felt his breath on her cheeks and looked up. His eyes were dark and confused. Her hair had come undone due to the impact. With one arm still supporting her, he tucked a recalcitrant tendril behind her ear. The touch of his cold fingers sent a shiver down her spine. That brought him out of the daze. He let go of her quickly and stepped back. She was shocked at what had just happened and how it made her feel. *Did he feel what she felt?*

'I am sorry. I tripped on the toolbox,' said Natasha, adjusting her jacket.

Veer seemed unaffected. 'No issues. Please be careful. Let's go now,' and he walked out.

Natasha followed Veer to the house sheepishly. She was still tingling all over from his touch. He, however, looked calm and composed. As they entered the house, he called out for Lydia and told her not to disturb him for the day. He would be working in his study. The pomegranate tree was completely forgotten.

Not knowing what to do, Natasha went to her room. Her wish of curling under the blanket was finally granted. She lay on the bed, hoping she would fall asleep, but her mind kept working, keeping sleep at bay. She was feeling things for Veer that she had never felt for anyone before. The way he tucked her hair behind her ear, and the way his finger lingered just below her ear, had awakened something inside her. She couldn't place the feeling, but she knew she hadn't felt half of what she was feeling now, when Yayu had kissed her. *If just the touch of his finger could make her feel like this, what if he kissed her?*

9

NATASHA WAS LOOKING at the majestic peaks as they glistened under the sun. Her five-feet-two frame looked beautiful, clad in a powder blue sari and sleeveless blouse. Her shoulder-length hair cascaded down in waves and diamonds glistened on her ears and on her neck. Her lovely eyes looked beautiful and her red lips parted slightly, as she took in the beauty of the scene. Veer came up from behind and put his left arm around her stomach, encircling her. His right hand bent her head to the left as his lips found the nape of her neck. An involuntary groan escaped Natasha.

She had closed her eyes and was about to place her lips on his lips, when a loud knock broke her reverie. She got up with a start. Lydia was knocking furiously to wake her up. Last night when she returned to her room, she had locked it involuntarily, lest she went out and acted on her heart's animalistic desires. She got up reluctantly and opened the door.

'Why weren't you responding? I got scared!' Lydia exclaimed as she made her way in with a tray laden with a coffee pot and biscuits. 'It has been snowing continuously since last night. Dadi was up the whole night, screaming with pain. I hope it stops snowing today or else it is going to be difficult,' she continued while making Natasha's bed and then turning on the geyser.

All Natasha wanted to do was to jump back into her cosy bed and forget about all her travails. She wondered if she would ever have the power to paint a rainbow on the sky by her sheer will. Accepting that she still lacked those superpowers, she decided to focus on what little she still had control on—her body and mind.

It was still snowing and she decided to go on a walk by herself. Maybe she would find inspiration for a painting or a sketch. If nothing, she could at least click a few pictures. She remembered how her Nani had once told her the story of when her mother had seen snow for the first time on their visit to Gulmarg. Nana had promised them a vacation in Kashmir if her mum scored high marks in her finals. As usual, her mum stood first in class and Nana had to take them to Kashmir. Nani told her that her mum was thirteen years old at that time. She had just started reading romantic novels and would also quote poets John Keats, Percy Shelley and William Wordsworth, when words failed her. On that particular occasion, when the beauty of the snow-clad mountains had filled her heart, her mother quoted Henry Longfellow, whom she had discovered during an inter-school poetry competition,

> Out of the bosom of the Air,
> Out of the cloud-folds of her garments shaken,
> Over the woodlands brown and bare,
> Over the harvest-fields forsaken,
> Silent, and soft, and slow
> Descends the snow.

Natasha repeated those words again and again as she got ready to go out for her walk. She was thinking of her mum and her Nani as she started walking. One snowflake landed on her nose and made her smile. She was still smiling when she came across a beautiful pine tree laden with snow. She wanted to shake the tree trunk so that all the snow would fall on her; she used to do that with the dew drops on tree leaves in JNU. She was still standing under the tree trying to reach a branch, when Veer's voice rang out, 'Behold her, single in the field...Yon solitary Highland Lass!'

She turned around smiling.

'I was trying to reach that branch,' she said sheepishly, pointing to a branch laden with snow.

'Oh, I will do that for you,' he said, and tugged at the branch. All the snow came crashing down on Natasha and she giggled with delight. There was snow on her cap, on her shoulders and on her boots. Some snow had also landed on her nose and she was trying to get it off with her gloved fingers.

Veer reached forward to brush the snowflakes away. She felt a jolt of electricity pass through her the moment his fingers touched her nose. She was pretty certain her nose and cheeks were pink with embarrassment. As she tried to compose herself, she lost balance and landed in his arms, again. This time, he didn't move away. He held her close to him and looked directly into her eyes. He brought his lips close to the nape of her neck and brushed it lightly with his lips. His warm breath sent tingling sensations down her spine.

He then moved closer to her ears and whispered, 'All I want to do is to take this snowball and put it inside your collar—like this,' and by the time she could react, he had put a snowball inside her clothes and run away. She shrieked as the snow trickled down, then gained her composure and made a big ball of snow and ran after him. They kept bombarding each other with snowballs as they ran towards the house. Veer ran inside first and vanished into his part of the house. Lydia had kept hot water for Natasha and that helped soothe her after an adrenaline-pumping session of playing like young children. The game of throwing snowballs was innocent and childlike, yet both of them knew that it was hardly friendly. It was sexually charged and waiting to explode. Natasha had never felt like this. When Veer was whispering in her ears, all she wanted was to give in to her basic instinct and kiss him. She was very disappointed when he didn't. *Would he judge her if he knew what she was thinking?*

10

VEER COULDN'T BELIEVE what he was feeling. *How could he let his guard down so much, with such a young girl!* She looked up to him as her mentor, her teacher, and all he could think about was taking her into his arms and kissing her till she asked for more. *What was wrong with him? Had he been away from female company for so long that even a young girl could turn him on? Could that be happening to him?* He was a mature, married man caught in the middle of very messy divorce proceedings; he couldn't be leading a young girl on like this. He had to get a grip on these crazy feelings…over his heart, which raced every time Natasha was around.

He had been smitten with her the moment he had seen her running towards his car on the highway. She was breathtakingly beautiful, with fear in her eyes and a sheen of perspiration on her flushed skin. He had been scared to death when she had fainted. He had tried to feel her pulse and hear her heartbeat. Once her well-being had been established, Veer had felt an instant attraction to her. When she had come to her senses, she had looked anxious, but she had calmed down when he had introduced himself. He liked that she had trusted him. He had dealt with so much negativity in his life that he really wanted someone to believe in him, look up to him. He didn't want her to fear him, and promised himself to keep his temper in check when dealing with her. He wanted to be in her good books. It was amazing how such a tiny person was able to illicit such strong feelings in him. He knew he was falling for her; he wanted to take that chance, but he would have to be careful.

Veer was still mulling over the happenings of the morning when he heard his mobile ringing. He couldn't believe he was hearing it ring. Finally, the network was available again. By the time he located it, the phone had stopped ringing. When he looked at it, there were hundreds of messages and notifications of calls he had missed. Many of them—including the most recent one—was from Amyra. *Why was Amyra trying to contact him?* He didn't want to waste his time thinking about all that. He was done with Amyra and anything to do with her. She had hurt him and used him in every manner possible. He had nothing left to give her. The loud knock on the door broke his reverie.

'Sir, Amyra Madam has called many times since the network came back. She is asking about your well-being and wants to talk to you. I have told her that you are well and very busy with work,' said Lydia, as she put down a tray laden with coffee and cookies.

'You did the right thing, Lydia. I don't want to talk to her,' replied Veer as he grabbed the cup of coffee with anger.

11

LYDIA WALKED INTO Natasha's room with a spring in her step. Natasha noticed the same and enquired, 'You look happy, Lydia. What's up?'

Lydia replied happily, 'Why not, Ma'am? Things are finally looking up for all of us. The phones started working today and the electricity is back. The radio and television are also working. Sir was able to get satellite signals for the set-top box and we are able to get the news of the world. It seems there was a cloudburst in Uttarkashi and there was large-scale destruction. Several thousands died, Ma'am—mostly pilgrims. It's very sad. You are definitely lucky to be alive. I had plugged your phone to charge while you were away. You can contact your friends and family as well,' she added.

That was too much information to absorb at once. The first thing that came to her mind was that she would have to leave now. But immediately, she thought that Veer had offered her an internship, followed by a job if all went well. She had to make sure that he would not go back on the offer. All of a sudden, the gloom of the weather looking up was replaced by the determination to stay put and learn from the master.

She needed to sort her mind and know exactly what she wanted. She first thought of calling Yayu and venting all her frustrations out on him, but she knew he would not listen to her. He would start talking immediately. She needed a saner voice, a person with more experience and a clearer head, who could guide her. So, she called Nani.

Nani picked up after the phone rang for a long time and started immediately. 'Natasha! How are you? Where are you, beta? I am so worried. Is everything okay? Are you alright? Where exactly are you?'

'Nani…Nani…hold on. One question at a time, please. I am alright. I am still where I was when I last spoke to you, at Bollywood film director Veer Singh Tomar's house. Finally, the network came back today so I could finally call you,' she replied, hoping that that would pacify Nani.

'Where did you say you were?' Nani asked.

'Oh, I thought I had informed you, Nani. I am at film director Veer Singh Tomar's house. And don't worry, I am not alone here. His grandmother and a housekeeper, Lydia, live with him. It is a very big house and I have been given my own room.'

'Are you sure you are okay, beta? On the news, we have been seeing the magnitude of the disaster and the number of people who have been affected. It's a very big tragedy. I was worried sick for your safety till you called the other day. Yayu has been a big support, telling me how capable you are of taking care of yourself. But you know, a mother's heart—or, for that matter, a Nani's heart,' she said, getting a bit emotional.

'Oh Nani…dear Nani…I am perfectly fine. In fact, I have called to sound you out on something I have been thinking. While I've been here, Veer has offered me an internship and an opportunity to work with him as an AD on his next film if the internship goes well,' she said, trying to contain her excitement.

'Go on,' said Nani, 'I feel there is more to this story.'

Nani knows me so well, Natasha thought to herself.

'I am really excited to be working with him, but…' she trailed off, wondering if she should let Nani in on this.

Nani nudged her on, 'Natasha, you can confide in me, beta. What is it? Tell me.'

That gave her confidence—the confidence she needed to unleash all that was within her heart.

'Nani, I am really attracted to him. I have never felt like this before. He is so charming, confident and sexy. I don't know if I will be able to handle it. I mean, it is the best thing that could have happened to me as far as my career is concerned but…what do you think?' she waited with bated breath.

Nani took her time to think about it. Her silence was making Natasha more anxious. She could hear Nani weighing the pros and cons, and she was dying to hear what she had to say. She knew Nani was very straightforward and didn't mince her words.

'Beta, how old is Veer?' Nani asked.

'Early thirties, Nani. I am guessing thirty-two or thirty-three.'

'Hmmm…' Nani gave nothing away. 'I remember reading about his divorce case and his abusive behaviour. What is your take on that?'

'Nani, I don't know much about that. We haven't talked about it. I know his divorce proceedings are going on and that he is in a mess, but that doesn't mean he is a bad person or that there is any truth to the crap the media has cooked up.' *Why was she defending him? Why did she want Nani to approve?* 'He is a nice guy, Nani. I know why you are asking me those questions but I need you to trust me,' she added passionately.

Nani had dealt with Natasha's mother enough to understand when to bow out.

'Beta, like you said, it is a very good career opportunity and you should make the most of it. I want you to be confident and receptive and learn as much as you can. This is what you always wanted. I believe in you but,' she then added tactfully, 'he is not a free man. I just want you to be careful. I don't want you to get hurt.'

'Yes, Nani, I understand. Accha, now tell me how have you been? Were you able to go for that play in Kamani Auditorium? How was it?' she asked, trying to digress from the topic.

'Yes, I went with Shama. It was very good. Anupam Kher was phenomenal. I missed you, beta. You would have loved it. After that, we went to Shama Aunty's place for dinner. Yayu joined us. He was very worried about you. Have you spoken to him yet?' Nani asked Natasha.

'No, Nani, I haven't. I will call him as soon as I can. Please don't tell him about Veer. I will tell him in detail myself,' she said, signing off.

Nani had made her point effectively and effortlessly. Even an hour after she had bid goodbye to Nani on the phone, Natasha was still thinking about what she had said. *He is not a free man.* Those words were echoing in her mind. *Should she speak to Yayu?* She was happy to hear that Shama Aunty, Yayu's mother, was keeping Nani company. *But should she tell Yayu? Would he understand?* She decided to postpone the matter till she could help it. One discussion with Nani was enough for the day. She had more delicious things to worry about and plan. She left the room, having put on a bright lip colour and an even brighter smile.

12

VEER WAS LOOKING irresistible in his khakis and an old, worn-out black hoodie. His dark hair was neatly tucked behind his ears and he was leaning over a couple of books, unaware of his devilish handsomeness. He was wearing a pair of spectacles and she could see the little boy of those pictures hanging in the gallery, hiding behind those glasses. She was still standing at the door of his study, when he looked up from the books and signalled her in. He had called her to the study to discuss work with her.

Natasha went in and took a seat on the opposite side of his office table. The table was made of hardwood. There were chequered boxes on the top, each filled with green leaves and a big glass covered it all. It was unique. She had never seen anything like that. The room had an aura of belonging to a man—a man's man. There were trophies and pictures and books and a small globe-like table near the window that overlooked the cliff. Trees and mountains covered in snow made a breathtakingly beautiful scene. The orangish-yellowish colours from the table lamp painted the room in a soft light.

She tried to look at the books he was reading—*A Doll's House* by Henrik Ibsen. She had read the book as a part of her course in her bachelors, and been very impressed with the thought-provoking play written in 1879. Ibsen had been able to give a voice to the main protagonist of the play, Nora, and had in fact given her courage to leave her husband.

She was still thinking about the play when Veer looked up and asked, 'Have you read the play?'

'Yes, I have.'

'What are your thoughts on the play?' he asked, trying not to focus on her red lips. She was looking very different with lipstick on. He couldn't decide if that difference was making him uncomfortable or excited.

'I had read it in the first year of my bachelors. I loved the main protagonist. Her courage and her integrity still resonate with me. Ibsen was a visionary. To come up with this play in that day and age was nothing less than revolutionary. In fact, I must tell you that I enacted the role of Nora in our annual play performance. I found it very liberating,' Natasha ended with a proud smile.

'Hmm,' Veer looked intently at her. Her eyes lit up whenever she talked about theatre or films. He could see the passion in her. 'I am delighted to know that you have not only read but also enacted the play. So, now that you are working as my intern, I want you to work on this play with me. I am trying to develop this story by setting it in an Indian context. I want to give my heroine hope and courage. I want to slam the door in the face of patriarchy as Nora leaves,' Veer said passionately.

Natasha was ecstatic at the prospect, but hid her glee.

'I would love to work on it. How shall we begin?'

'Let's first work on the background a little,' he said, sounding pedantic, 'and, then, with the main characters. Your job for today is to think about the kind of family your heroine would come from, what characteristics she would have and if she would be married,' he said, standing up. 'I have some work to finish, so I will meet you at dinner. You can use the computer in the library and all the books there are at your disposal.'

Then he put his hand forward for a handshake, as if to seal the deal. She took the hand he offered and shook it. She looked at him; he looked confused. She lingered longer than she should have, and didn't want to let go. He was not letting go either.

And then he did. She left the room as quickly as she could. She felt flustered. *Did he know that she wanted to kiss him so badly that it was driving her nuts?* She had seen him look at her lips briefly. *Did he feel what she felt?*

13

'MADE FOR EACH other'

Amyra and Veer looked perfect on the red carpet at the Filmfare Award function. The much-in-love couple walked hand in hand as the shutterbugs went crazy to capture the moment. Amyra looked divine in a Manish Malhotra ensemble. Veer looked at her with adoration. He casually pulled her closer and kissed on her lips as they made their way inside. Later, as Veer was announced the winner of the Best Director Award, Amyra looked at him with lot of affection and a 'we did it' smile. Their chemistry and public display of affection made a lot of people uncomfortable but we are delighted in their happiness!

Natasha had meandered from one book to another and finally started researching on the computer in the library. She was looking for an interesting background to place her protagonist in, and couldn't remember when she typed Veer's name in the unsuspecting search engine. Her heart skipped a beat as various pictures of Veer with Amyra popped up on the screen. She knew Amyra was gorgeous, but Natasha had never really bothered to see her pictures closely. Amyra was exquisite. She reminded her of Madhubala and Madhuri Dixit. Her smile started from her lips and spread to her eyes.

Natasha knew that stars had a big entourage when it came to their makeup and their dresses, but she was surprised at how casual and chic Amyra looked in her pictures where she was with underprivileged children, and how sombre she looked while volunteering with the wives of soldiers of the Indian Army.

In the pictures where Veer and Amyra were together, they looked fabulous. She was nearly as tall as him, in heels, yet she looked very coy and feminine with him around. There was an aura of love and devotion in all their pictures. In most of them, he was holding her hands possessively. Natasha wondered what could have gone wrong to split them up and make them go public with their problems. As she was reading through all the news items available on the net, about their marital discord, she realized that only Amyra had been quoted in all. Veer had never been quoted by anyone. He had never given his side of the story.

There were many articles maligning him, but not even one defending him. Some big names from the movie industry had come out in his support but he had never cleared his position in public. In the more recent articles, it was written, 'Veer had promised to give Amyra whatever she wanted if she let go of all the cases that she had filed against him.' *What had he done? What did he have to hide? Why wasn't Veer defending himself?*

She was so lost in all her 'research' that she lost track of time. When she looked at her phone, which she had kept on silent, she saw five missed calls from Yayu. She knew she had to speak to him that day, or God knows he would land up in Landour! She couldn't risk that. Still, she didn't want to talk to Yayu yet. Her mind was filled with Veer. She couldn't place the feeling, but she could feel her heart skipping a beat when she looked at his pictures. She felt a little angry when she saw Amyra and Veer together. She didn't want to think about them but she couldn't seem to let go either.

She looked at the notes she had made. It was not too much. She would have to work harder at her internship if she wanted to impress Veer. She decided to block all the images of Amyra and Veer from her mind and continued working on the assignment he had given her. She knew he would ask her at the end of the day and she couldn't disappoint him.

After two hours of undisturbed hard work, Natasha knew her heroine's story, where she came from, and that she would be a fighter with a very privileged background. Natasha also knew that she would be courageous. She knew where she would place the story but she had not decided on the name yet—she just couldn't.

Lydia walked in with coffee and cookies as she was shutting off the computer.

'Long day, Ma'am? Lots of work today.'

'Yes, Lydia. Finally have something to show for the day,' Natasha said happily.

'Ma'am, Veer Sir had called. He has asked me to tell you to meet him for dinner at Marriot at 8 p.m. He will meet you there. The driver will take you,' Lydia informed Natasha before leaving the room.

Natasha was very excited at the prospect. *Why was Veer meeting her there? What would she wear?* She suddenly panicked. Thank God she had packed some dresses and saris. Nani had insisted on packing some formal and some dressy things. *Nani was the best!* She left the coffee halfway and ran towards her room to get ready.

After an hour of great indecision about what to wear, which colour of lipstick to put and whether to wear her hair down or not, Natasha finally decided that she looked fabulous; she was ready to go. She was wearing an off-shoulder black dress that ended just above her knees. Tights and a wrap completed her look. Her hair gleamed with health and her fuschia lips looked absolutely kissable. Her boots gave her the advantage of height and added to her gait. She looked adorable and sexy at the same time. While on her way out, she met Lydia, who looked positively shocked at her transformation.

'Ma'am, you look irresistible!' she exclaimed.

Would Veer find her irresistible?

14

NATASHA FELT CONFIDENT that he would take notice. As the car meandered through the heavily snowed-covered roads of Landour, her heart was beating faster than ever before. She was trying to catch her breath as the driver said, 'Here we are, Madam,' as they entered the magnanimous foyer of the five-star hotel. The place reeked of luxury. As she stepped down from the car, a valet was there to assist her and the doorman opened the door for her. Right across from the entrance, in the middle of the regal receiving area, stood Veer—looking royal. She knew why he was a celebrity and she was a commoner. At six-feet-plus height, the man was towering over his surroundings. He was wearing a black suit with a white shirt and a pink tie. The cut of his suit, the quality of the cloth and how he carried it made a lot of difference. And the fact that he worked out added to the oomph factor, so to say. *He was,* she thought shyly, *extremely sexy*.

He was talking to a group of well-dressed gentlemen. It looked like a business meeting that was about to wrap up. As she was walking towards him, he looked up, looked stunned for a second and then waved her over. By the time she reached him, he had bid goodbye to his company and was alone.

'Hi,' she said, trying to sound confident, when she was actually feeling like a mess. He looked like he belonged here; she, on the other hand, was a misfit. She hoped that he wouldn't mind her clothes too much. *She had seen his pictures and knew what standards he was used to*, she thought, recalling Amyra and her exquisite fashion sense.

'Hello,' he said stoically, 'you look different.'

She did. Veer thought the makeup and dress added a sexy edge to her charm. She looked so tempting that he was afraid he wouldn't be able to keep his hands off her. He placed his hand on the small of her back as he led her towards the restaurant. This innocent act of social courtesy sent shivers down her spine.

He had arranged for them to have dinner at his 'usual' table, as the maître d' pointed out. Natasha was a fairly confident girl, yet all this made her nervous. *Did she look okay? Was she underdressed for the place? Was she overdressed?* Her mind was working so fast that she hadn't heard him asking if she was okay. He called her name.

'Natasha... where are you? You were miles away,' he said, offering her the drinks menu.

'No... no,' she replied, flustered, trying to decide on a drink. 'I will have a vodka with tonic and lemon.'

'Good choice, and what about starters?'

'Anything you like! Vegetarian though,' she replied.

It was a beautiful setting. Veer had chosen a corner table with a view of the snow-clad, moonlit mountains.

'So, did you make any progress with your work today?' asked Veer.

'Yes. I have searched extensively for the background of the protagonist. I feel I am ready with that, at least. Do you want me to brief you?'

'No…no…I would like to see the final result in writing,' he replied, dismissing her. 'I want to know about you today. Tell me about who Natasha is,' he added with a smile.

She looked at him with surprise. She hadn't expected him to be interested in her life. She had imagined herself telling him about her life many a times, but now that he had asked, she didn't know where to begin. 'As I told you and Dadi earlier, I'm from a middle-class Punjabi family in Delhi. After losing my parents at a young age, I grew up with a loving grandmother, much like yours—my Nani. She is the heart and soul of my family. She teaches in JNU and has a free soul. I am whatever I am today because of her care and affection. Even when I was coming here for this internship, she was sceptical but jumped on board the moment I asked her to believe in me and that I knew the internship would propel me in the right direction in my career…' she trailed off.

Veer was looking at her intently. 'How about when you told her about me?'

'She was not very easy to convince,' Natasha confessed with a twinkle in her eyes, 'but I told her that you were an alumnus of our alma mater and wouldn't bite.'

Veer laughed out loud and said, 'I want to know about you, Natasha. What makes you Natasha?'

She had thought of this many a times and the answer came very quickly.

'Veer, the absence of my parents in my life, makes me Natasha. It made me self-reliant and independent even at a very young age. Nani was always around but there were days when I wondered about my parents and what would have happened if they were around. My father's side didn't want me when I was a baby, but once my Dada was on his deathbed, they fought a very difficult battle for my custody. I prayed every day that Nani would get to keep me, but when I met my Dadi, I could see some of my father in her and wanted to hold on. Nani never stopped me, but they passed away one after the other, leaving a vacuum in my life. I have learnt to live with absences. Yet, I like to dream of a perfect future, with a big family,' she said, her eyes glistening.

The waiter chose this very moment to deliver their starters and drinks. Natasha noticed how Veer engaged the waiter. He not only helped him with the dishes, he asked about his health and also that of his family. He enquired about his son's admission and informed him that he had put in a good word with the school principal. Veer's eyes were filled with kindness as he addressed the young waiter, Ramesh. Ramesh was brimming with confidence by the time he left. Natasha realized that Veer was more likely 'sinned against' than 'sinning'. He was a very warm person and took genuine interest in people's lives. She could see that the media reports about his violent nature and domestic abuse couldn't be true. There had to be more to it.

'So, where were we?' Veer asked.

'I was telling you how I convinced Nani to let me intern for you and you found it quite amusing,' Natasha replied, adjusting her bra strap involuntary. She realized what she was doing only when she saw Veer's eyes move in that direction. She removed her hands quickly and asked Veer, 'What about you? Tell me something about your life, your parents, your childhood.'

'I was born with a metaphorical silver spoon. My parents were childhood friends, who got married very young. They were very generous and were known for their philanthropy. My grandfather was an industrialist and my mother was the daughter of his business partner. My parents lived in Delhi and were the toast of every party. They were loved wherever they went. After many years of their marriage when they had me, they gave up their social engagements to spend time with me. I had a very happy childhood.'

'And then?'

'And then when I was in third year of college, my parents met with an accident and died. My life turned upside down. I was not ready for the kind of grief I felt after their death. I couldn't move; I would sleep for days together. My Dadi was instrumental in bringing me back to reality. She was from an undivided India and had endured the Partition. She had dealt with multiple losses over the years and her wisdom and love got me through the worst time of my life,' he said with sadness in his eyes.

Ramesh came forward to repeat the drinks and gave both of them some welcome respite from a very emotional moment. Veer realized that he had let his guard down. *This girl was making him talk—too much!* He never revealed so much of himself to anyone so quickly. He was confused with how easily she could get that done. Her loss and life had been similar to his and maybe that was the reason he opened up to her. She could understand what he was talking about. Natasha, on the other hand, was feeling very vulnerable. She wanted to hug him and tell him that she understood his pain and had been through the same, but words failed her. She excused herself and went to the loo to compose herself.

By the time she came back, the moment had passed and both of them were ready for the entrées. The food was delicious and the ambience added to it. When the maître d' came forward with the last course of the meal, Natasha checked the time. It was way past midnight. So much time had gone by and she was still having fun. She was a little tipsy by the time dinner ended. After two drinks, she had wanted to stop, but she just didn't. She was enjoying the dinner, the conversation and her handsome partner; she let go of her inhibitions. From family talk to talking about films and film stars, cricket and cricket stars, books and Mussoorie, they just kept going on.

She didn't realize when, but Veer was holding her hand and leading her up the stairs. 'Where are you taking me?' she asked, giggling like a school girl.

'Shhhh...' he put his finger to her lips, 'Quiet, girl. You will love it. Just follow my lead.'

She complied.

'Here it is,' he signalled towards an assortment of swings and playthings. One would have thought that having swings on the roof, in a city where it snows so much, would be absolutely impractical, but Natasha could see the logic in it. The glass roof overhead kept them protected from the snow, but the open sides let the freshness and crispness of the cool air come in. She could see moonlight bouncing off the snow-covered peaks. She was sure the view would be even more mesmerizing in the daylight. He walked forward and asked her to sit down on one of the swings.

'Hold on,' he said as he gave her a push.

She went up high, cold wind kissing her cheeks. He pushed again and she went higher. She felt like she was flying. It was amazing.

'I love it,' she screamed with delight.

After a few minutes, he stopped pushing and as she slowed down, he came and stood in front of her. She got up from the swing and stumbled right into his arms.

He smelled delicious—manly and clean. She put both her hands on his chest and rested her head on it, where his heart was.

She could feel his heart pounding. His hands were resting on the small of her back. She had closed her eyes and was desperately trying to control herself when she felt his hand come up to her cheek. He lightly ran his fingers through her hair; some hair ran astray from where she had secured them with pins. She wanted to kiss him. She wanted him to kiss her. He could sense that and cut it short. He kissed her on her head and said, 'Let's go. You are very sleepy.'

His car was waiting at the foyer. He opened the door for her, made her comfortable and then came to the driver's seat.

'Are you okay?' he asked, before inserting the key in the ignition. She nodded in agreement. She was still thinking about him kissing her. The journey back to the bungalow was fast and over before she could decide if she should put her hand on his thigh or not.

When he opened the door for her, she came out feeling a little angry at herself for being so indecisive. He took the keys from his pocket and opened the door as she stood behind him. Once inside, she turned around to thank him.

'I loved hanging out with you. It was "surreal but nice",' she said, quoting *Notting Hill*, which they had talked about as being their all-time favourite romantic movie.

He smiled. 'I loved it too. I have been so carefree after a very long time. So, thank you for being a perfect date.'

'Were we on a date?'

'Yes,' he answered with a devilish glint in his eyes.

'How do you generally end a date?' Natasha asked, feeling bold.

They were standing just outside her room. The gallery was gently lit up. Veer looked handsome beyond words. He was loosening his scarf with one hand and taking off his gloves at the same time. Natasha was looking at him with anticipation. He looked directly in her eyes and moved closer. He kept moving closer till his lips were inches apart from hers. He put his hands on the small of her back and gently put his lips on hers. Her lips parted in a gasp and he used this moment to gently touch her tongue with his. She responded by tilting her head and giving him deeper access. Greedy for more, he ventured further and was greeted by the deliciousness of her response. She put her hand behind his head and asked for more. He was not ready for this. He got lost in her supple lips and her perfect body as his hand slipped further to her bottom and he pressed her to him. She pressed her breasts against his chest and demanded more. She leaned against the wall and hit a picture hanging there. The crashing sound of the glass jolted them back into reality. He let her go immediately, and without realizing what she was doing, she went inside her room, leaving him standing there, confused.

Natasha hurried inside her room and bolted the door. Her breathing was very fast and her palms were sweating. With one hand on her chest, she reached for the switch to turn on the light. The orange glow of the lamp filled the room with warmth. Her eyes were closed. She could still see him right in front of her. He was coming closer and closer and closer still, till she felt his breath on her lips. The bag in her other hand hit the ground with a thud and jolted her back to reality. She opened her eyes with reluctance.

She saw her reflection in the mirror over the fireplace. Her lips looked swollen. Her lipstick was a very dull colour now—so much for the non-transfer claim she had paid for. Her hair was loosening from the numerous pins she had put. Her vision was a little hazy and she was a bit drunk. Natasha walked towards the bed and fell on it. She had pulled her boots off somewhere in the corridor; she didn't remember where. Veer had tried to catch hold of her as she had stumbled across it, but she hadn't let him, having run away.

She fell asleep while trying to read the text message on her phone.

15

AFTER A FITFUL night, Natasha woke up to a cacophony of birds trying to tell her that it was time to wake up. She was still in between slumber and complete consciousness when she heard the faint buzzing of her phone. Startled, she began looking for it frantically. She finally located it under the covers. There were twenty missed calls and ten messages—all from Yayu. She was trying to read the messages when Yayu called again.

'Hello, Natasha... Hello... Hello,' he said frantically.

'Hey, Yayu... *Kya haal hain*? How are you?'

'Natasha... where are you, yaar? I've been so worried. You haven't taken my calls or replied to my messages... What is going on? Are you okay?' he sounded concerned.

'Yes, I am absolutely fine. I was sleeping. You tell me, what's so urgent?'

'Well, I am here in Landour and I am trying to locate you. Nani gave me incomplete directions...' Yayu was still going on, but Natasha was not listening.

Shit! Why was he here? What was he doing here? She remembered her kiss with Veer last night and her stomach flipped. *What was she going to say to him? Yayu will realize something was different. What will Veer think about Yayu?*

'Hey, are you there? Natasha ... tell me where exactly you are staying so I can come there ASAP,' said Yayu, getting impatient. 'I have taken up a room near Library Chowk in Mussoorie. It's cheaper.'

'I know how cheap you are, Yayu. No need to point it out,' said Natasha, trying to play along. 'Come to Landour. I will meet you at Char Dukan. And now I am going to get ready, so put the phone down,' she said, and cut the call.

She was still thinking about the kiss. *What if her lips were swollen?* She felt like they were. *Would Yayu notice the difference? Should she tell him about her feelings towards Veer?*

Veer was an awesome kisser. She had been kissed before but not like last night. He had consumed her. He had possessed her. She wanted so much more than that. If that photo had not fallen, who knows what would have happened! She was certain that she would have given in to the temptation. The fact that he was not a free man should have had some bearing on her, but surprisingly it didn't. She didn't want to think. She just wanted to let things happen. *Did Veer like her as much?* He was attracted to her, that was for sure. Hopefully, he didn't regret kissing her. She wanted to avoid meeting him today; it would be awkward. After being so intimate last night, what would she say to him across the breakfast table. *She would try to get out without meeting him,* she decided.

She was just getting out of the room when she bumped into Lydia.

'Oh careful, Ma'am,' said Lydia, adjusting the tray carrying her breakfast. 'Don't you want breakfast?'

Natasha adjusted her bag and said, 'No, Lydia. I am meeting a friend for breakfast at Char Dukan. But why were you bringing it to my room? I would have come down,' she added guiltily.

'No problem, Ma'am. Veer Sir had told me to take the breakfast to your room.'

'Oh, did he?' *And here she was thinking he liked her.* She felt her heart break a little. 'Did he say anything else? Where is he?'

'Ma'am, he left very early in the morning. He took a bag with him. He met Dadi before he left, so she might know if he will be back by the evening. He asked me to give you this book.'

Lydia handed over a copy of *Love Letters of Great Men.* It did not seem to be marked. Nothing was written on it other than on the first page:

Dear Veer,

Learn from the masters!

~Amyra

She felt like a train had just run her over. *What did he mean by this? Did he want her to know that Amyra was still a part of his life?* She kept the book in her bag and left the house quickly to meet Yayu.

16

VEER WAS THE quintessential male. He didn't waste even a second in running away from a situation that was proving to be too much for him emotionally. He was feeling overwhelmed with all that was happening. He had left early in the morning for Dehradun. He didn't know if he could accomplish something, but he needed to be away to sort his head. He was still going over the happenings of last night. They had a fantastic date, a meaningful conversation, beautiful company and he was a gentleman throughout. Yet, he let his basic instinct take over. He didn't think; he just responded to her. It had been a while since he had kissed anyone, but the way she reacted to his simple kiss made him let go. He wanted so much more.

Veer was still standing in the corridor when Natasha went inside and closed the door with a bang. He came forward to knock on the door but held back just in time. *What was he doing?* This girl was driving him crazy. She was so innocent but acted so grown-up, that he forgot how inexperienced she was. She was his apprentice. But he could not deny how much he was attracted to her. He liked the way she was so full of life. Her eyes lit up when she talked about movies. She reminded him of his youth. He was as passionate about movies and movie-making in his youth. She was all heart and he could see that in her big, expressive eyes. He didn't want to lead her on. *What could he offer her?* He was still a married man, battling charges of sexual abuse and wife battery. But there was something about this girl, which made him forget all his blues and want to fall in love. *Love?* He checked himself. *It couldn't be love. It has to be something else.*

He had left the book, *Love letters of Great Men,* for Natasha because he wanted her to read that page he had marked. He wanted her to know what that kiss meant to him. But he had forgotten about the dedication on the first page. When he remembered it, he cursed himself. *What would Natasha think? Why had he left a book given to him by his wife for her?* He should have left flowers or a memento, or just stayed back himself.

But he couldn't. He just had to run, lest he end up making a bigger fool of himself. *Why did he leave the book for her?* He could only hope that she would see beyond the first page. Like so many other things in his life, he could only hope that it would go well.

The journey to Dehradun from Landour via Mussoorie is nearly an hour and a half, but it took him three hours to cover that distance. Not only was he driving slowly because of the weather, the happenings of the night, interspersed with flashes of his past, kept slowing him further. He had organized a meeting with his lawyer to figure out how he could get out of this messy business of his failed marriage. He had not given any thought to his court case and his wife for a while, but in the last few days he had been feeling the need to be rid of it. Natasha made him look forward in life and that meant letting go of his past.

He had met Amyra at a very vulnerable stage in his life. He was still not over the pain of losing his parents when she had strutted into his life. She always wore high heels to add to her very tall frame of five feet, nine inches. Veer had been attracted to her initially because she was already a famous model and a leggy beauty, but he was later consumed with his love for her because of how she helped him cope with his pain. She was the muse to the creative in him. Together, they achieved many laurels and attained many heights. Getting married was the next logical step and they followed through. Veer came from a very happy home and wanted to make one of his own with Amyra.

He was just out of college when he had first met Amyra at a friend's party. She was an established model by then. He was a potential filmmaker. He was sitting in a corner, nursing his broken heart, with a drink in his hand. His parents had been gone for six months then and this was the first time he had come to a party. Amyra happened to be there because she was the showstopper for the fashion week in Delhi. When she saw him, her heart lurched and she walked up to him. 'Hey, are you a model?' she asked him, knowing very well that he wasn't. He looked up and said, 'No'. He looked unfazed but he was shaken. He had seen Amyra's advertisements; he knew who she was. 'You have got the looks,' Amyra said with a smile. By the end of the evening, Amyra had offered to drop him home but he never went home. He went to her hotel room and they talked through the night. Veer had not been able to talk about his loss to anyone except his Dadi, who could only do so much as she was also dealing with losing her son and beloved daughter-in-law. When Amyra asked him about the reason for the sadness in his eyes, he let go and poured his heart out to her. She had been through the same at a younger age and knew how to comfort him. The friendship that began that night anchored Veer's life, personally and professionally.

When Veer came over to Mumbai on Amyra's insistence, she introduced him to all his friends and peers. She also got him a meeting with a big production house that was launching her. It was that meeting that landed him a three-movie contract. She worked in his first movie and it was a super-duper hit. Their careers in the film industry began together. Then they continued making a lot of movies together, most of which did well at the box office.

They had been together for nearly ten years by then and were a so-called power couple in Bollywood, but like all good things that come to an end, their relationship started facing hardships. Somehow, somewhere, the love and the ease in their relationship vanished. Veer became more and more involved with his craft and she was travelling most of the time to various locations for shooting. Since there appearances together in public decreased, the media started talking about the troubled waters that their relationship was in and both of them succumbed to it. They started having fights about what the media was reporting and why Amyra was being linked to her co-star, Ranbir. Veer believed that he was not the jealous types, but he was surprised at how his heart and mind reacted to his wife being linked to someone else. He was very possessive about her and that made him extremely angry—so much so, that he screamed at her at a party and nearly hit her in full media presence. That was the end of their relationship and the beginning of this messy divorce proceeding.

The last movie that they had worked together on had been a commercial and a critical success. There were talks of him getting the National Award for Best Direction finally after so many years of slogging it out. He was on a professional high when the rumours of Amyra and Ranbir started doing the rounds. They had been shooting for a month in Bhuj, Gujarat, for a movie, and were not reachable. Amyra would call up whenever she had the time. Once, when she called, Veer asked about Ranbir and her reply was not satisfactory. He headed there in two days to check on them himself, and realized the rumours were correct. Amyra didn't negate them either. He became angry and left. She didn't follow him.

When the shoot was over and she came back to Mumbai, she went to stay with Ranbir instead of returning home to Veer. Veer met her at a party and lost his cool. He screamed at her and had nearly hit her, when his friends pulled him away. That was what everybody saw and the media reported. Ranbir added fuel to the fire by holding a press conference to confirm that Amyra wanted to get out of her abusive marriage and through all this, Amyra kept quiet. She filed for divorce and asked for a very big alimony. Veer was hurt with Amyra's behaviour, and sad that she had chosen to end their marriage the way that she did, but he didn't put up a fight. He just left town and came to Mussoorie to be with his grandmother. He sent out feelers for his new script and found takers with whom he was now negotiating. The National Award was announced in the meantime and he was propelled into limelight once again. That is when Amyra started reaching out to him.

He was meandering down the mountain, navigating the loopy roads when Amyra called him. He didn't take her call. She called again. He let it ring. She called again. He got irritated but still didn't take the call. She eventually stopped calling. Now, there was a message from her. He didn't read it. He reached his townhouse in Doon and asked the cook to set breakfast for him. Then he took a quick shower and called his lawyer.

17

CHAR DUKAN WAS the place to hang out in Landour. As the name suggested, it was a cluster of four shops near a quaint little church. The church, along with the beauty of the hills, made for a picturesque setting. The twin towns of Mussoorie and Landour were very important to the British while they ruled India. It was the perfect getaway from the heat of the plains and to hide away any wild oats that they might have sown, in the numerous residential schools. Surrounded by all this glory, Yayu looked handsome. *Had he lost some weight?* she wondered. Natasha ran the last few metres. She was disappointed in Veer's behaviour, but she was determined to not let it spoil her mood; not when her best friend was visiting her.

Yayu was facing away from her he hadn't seen her approaching. Natasha went from behind him, put her arms around him and bumped her head against his in sisterly affection.

'Natasha!' he turned around.

'Yayu, I missed you, yaar.' They hugged. Natasha felt a tug at her heartstrings. The comfort of familiarity got the better of her, and she felt very emotional.

'If only this was love, Natasha,' Yayu teased her.

'Come on, Yayu! Don't be so mean,' Natasha slapped his back lovingly.

'So, what have you been hiding from me?' Yayu asked point-blank.

'Arre... I will tell you everything, but let's order something to eat first. I am famished.'

Char Dukan's tea and coffee shops also offered delicious breakfast options like waffles, pancakes and the good old Maggi and bread-omelette. Chairs and tables were kept very close to each other and if you wanted, you could eavesdrop into the conversation on the other table very easily. Yayu signalled the waiter and asked him to get Maggi, bread-omelette and a pot of coffee. While breakfast was being prepared, Natasha caught up on the happenings of Delhi and their friends.

'You look very happy,' Natasha commented when Yayu was describing his date with Shanaya.

'*Unke aane se aajati hai chehre par raunak, to woh samajhte hain bimar ka haal accha hai,*' replied Yayu, being Yayu.

Over breakfast, Natasha told Yayu all about her adventures and her meeting with Veer. He was very interested in the way Veer worked at his craft. He asked her various questions on what she thought was his USP. He also enquired about his personality and also his personal life. He asked about Amyra and also if they were still in love. He wanted to meet Veer and, of course, was curious of her assessment of him. She tried to keep it as unemotional as possible so Yayu wouldn't guess that Natasha had any feelings towards him, but best friends are best friends after all.

'So, you have fallen in love with him,' Yayu declared.

Love? No, not love. Love? Can that be? Love? Maybe! Natasha felt her heart racing. *She had not thought about love. Veer was alpha male, handsome, intelligent, sexy, creative—but taken. She should not fall in love with him, but what if she had? He was passionate; she had seen that last night, but should she let herself get carried away?*

'No, I am not in love with him,' she replied firmly. 'I like him. He is my mentor. But there are no feelings involved,' she said, looking away.

'Okay, so you are not in love with him but when do I get to meet him? He is from my alma mater, too, you know,' he added, a smile lurking on his lips.

'Hopefully soon, but he is out of town today, so we will do touristy things today. I am scouting for locations for the setting of the script he has me working on, and I want to check out a few places. I will work while you play. Let's go to Kempty Falls,' she said, picking up her bag from the table. On Yayu's insistence, Natasha told him about the script and was pleasantly surprised at Yayu's insight. While they were walking to Kempty, she kept noting down the points in the notepad app in her phone.

Yayu was his hilarious best and Natasha forgot all her troubles in all the fun they had. From the semi-frozen Kempty Falls to Gun Hill, they roamed through the day, eating Tibetan delicacies and sipping on hot coffee. She also found a commentary on Ibsen's *A Doll's House*, which she picked up from a pretty little bookshop. Natasha bought a lot of knick-knacks from the flea market, including a Bhutiya shawl for Nani and a muffler for Yayu. The day couldn't have been better spent. After dinner at a local kiosk, when Yayu asked her about where he could drop her, she said she wanted to stay back. Yayu pointed out that not only was it a little inappropriate now that he had a girlfriend, he also said that his room was not good enough for her to stay. Natasha knew how important her work was, but the girl in her—who had a huge crush on a boy who was avoiding her—didn't want to go back. She didn't want to face Veer. She didn't want to face the fact that she had let him see the real her and he didn't care.

'What is going on, Natasha? You can tell me.' Yayu could see the tension on her face.

'It's nothing. I am just worried about my work. I can take a taxi from here. You rest. You have had a long day. What time shall we meet up tomorrow?' Natasha changed the topic.

Yayu didn't pester her. 'I will call you in the morning to fix up.'

Natasha reached Veer's bungalow in half an hour to find his car parked in the foyer.

18

NATASHA HAD GONE to her room without making any noise, firstly, because it was late and secondly, because she didn't want to bump into Veer. Once in her room, she changed into comfortable clothes and decided to look into the book he had left for her. Lying under multiple layers of bohemian duvets, surrounded by the orangish hue of the lamp, Natasha read the name of the book out loud: 'Love Letters of Great Men'. She was reading the preface and wondered why he had left her that book. One of the pages of the book was dog-eared and she immediately turned to that page. *Had he marked that page for her?* It was a letter from the celebrated dramatist, William Congreve, to his beloved, Arabella Hunt, written in the seventeenth century.

To Mrs Arabella Hunt

Dear Madam,

–Not believe that I love you? You cannot pretend to be so incredulous. If you do not believe my tongue, consult my eyes, consult your own. You will find by yours that they have charms; by mine that I have a heart which feels them. Recall to mind what happened last night. That at least was a lover's

> kiss. Its eagerness, its fierceness, its warmth, expressed the God its parent. But oh! Its sweetness, and its melting softness expressed Him more. With trembling in my limbs, and fevers in my soul, I ravish'd it. Convulsions, pantings, murmurings showed the mighty disorder within me: the mighty disorder increased by it. For those dear lips shot through my heart, and thro' my bleeding vitals, delicious poison, and an avoidless but yet a charming ruin.
>
> What cannot a day produce? The night before I thought myself a happy man, in want of nothing, and in fairest expectation of fortune; approved of by men of wit, and applauded by others. Pleased, nay, charmed with my friends, my then dearest friends, sensible of every delicate pleasure, and in their turns possessing all.
>
> But Love, almighty Love, seems in a moment to have removed me to a prodigious distance from every object but you alone. In the midst of crowds I remain in solitude. Nothing but you can lay hold of my mind, and that can lay hold of nothing but you. I appear transported to some foreign desert with you (oh! That I were really thus transported!)...

She didn't read any further. Her heart was racing. That beautiful description of 'last night's kiss' took her breath away. It was an earth-moving kiss that left her with no sense of time and space. She did feel transported. The letter echoed her feelings—the softness, the sweetness and the passion of the kiss did leave her wanting for more. She did feel her body heat up as she closed her eyes and reminisced about the happenings of last night. *But what did he feel? Did he want her to read this? Did he feel like Congreve, or was this by chance?*

19

'NATASHA,' SHE HEARD Dadi call her from the breakfast table. She was trying to get away from the house without being noticed, but had to keep a copy of her research in Veer's study. That's when Dadi saw her. Veer was sitting next to her, reading the newspaper. *What would he say?* He looked gorgeous in a beige high-neck sweater and blue jeans. His hair was still wet from the shower. He didn't look up when Dadi called out to her. Dadi looked healthier than the last few days. Maybe that was why she was having breakfast in the dining room and not on her bed.

'Good morning, Dadi. You look fresh!' She ignored Veer. *If he wanted to talk, he would have to make the effort.*

'Natasha, Lydia told me that one of your friends is here,' Dadi asked, as Natasha put some poha on her plate. Veer signalled Lydia to pour a cup of coffee for Natasha.

'Yes, Dadi, my best friend Yayu is here. He is putting up at a hotel at Library Point. I asked him to shift to Landour, but he said he was on a budget. I was going to meet him now. We plan to go to Lal Tibba today.'

'Veer, what are you doing today? Actually, I don't care what you are doing. Take time out in the evening as Natasha is going to bring Yayu over for dinner,' Dadi declared. Veer kept his fork down and looked at Dadi, visibly piqued, though he held back.

Natasha didn't want to impose. 'Oh please, Dadi. You don't have to do that. I will go and meet him anyway. He will be off to Delhi tomorrow. I don't want to inconvenience you or Veer.'

'It's not an imposition,' Veer spoke for the first time since she had sat down on the table for breakfast. 'I will be here, Dadi, and in fact, you are welcome to have one of the cars from the garage,' he looked at Natasha now, 'Ram Singh can drive you around and bring you guys over for dinner in the evening.'

'So, it's final. Natasha, we will see you and Yayu here at 7 sharp. By the way, Natasha, is Yayu "the one"?' Dadi winked.

Veer was looking very intently at Natasha's face. She could hear her heart beating. The way he was looking at her was making her uncomfortable. She knew that she should not lie but she did want to ruffle his feathers and see if he would react at all.

'I don't know if he is the one, Dadi, but he has always been around, through thick and thin. He gives me strength to carry on when I am down and out. He looks out for my Nani when I am not around. He is possessive about me and I appreciate how much pains he takes to look after me. I do love him, Dadi,' she added with conviction.

Veer didn't react, but asked Lydia to have the car brought out in the foyer. Dadi was kinder. She said that she was not only happy that Natasha had somebody like Yayu to fall back on, but that she was really looking forward to hosting him in the evening.

Natasha was secretly hoping that Veer would follow her up to the foyer and say something. But he didn't. He just nodded at her when she asked to be excused for her meeting with Yayu. *Did he really not care?* She thought that he had wanted her to read that love letter, he had wanted her to know what he felt about their kiss that night, but it seemed otherwise. He had not made any attempt to speak to her since that night. She was now convinced that he didn't mean anything by giving her the book.

Her thoughts kept going back to that beautiful night, lovely dinner and the passionate kiss that had rocked her world. He was the perfect gentleman that day, even when she had wanted to kiss him on the roof, he had held her like a friend and didn't take advantage of her drunkenness. What triggered that passion in him an hour later, she couldn't decipher. She was asking for it, she knew. She was deliberately being bold and was pushing him to make a move, but when he did make a move, she was not ready for what hit her. She had never experienced such surge of passion and excitement that made her whole body tingle. She could still feel the sensation in the pit of her stomach and the tips of her nipples. She let the memory take her over as she closed her eyes.

'Madam, we are here,' Ram Singh opened the door.

She then looked at her phone and saw two missed calls from Yayu. She dialled his number to locate him. Ram Singh had driven to Library Point as directed.

Yayu picked up in two rings and said, 'I am right in front of you.'

She looked up and saw him waving at her. She got down from the car, went to him, and hugged him tight. There was such comfort in familiarity. Yayu represented all that was stable in her life, all that was a given—her Nani's love, Yayu's friendship, her room in her home, her memories that couldn't be taken away from her. Natasha was not ready for any more upheavals. She wanted stability and surety. *She could not get that from a married man and she would not compromise on her happiness. What the hell! She would just focus on learning the craft from him. She should not let her heart get in the way of her career. She should be grown-up about such things. Such emotional accidents happen and people move on. She would not let Veer know that he had affected her at all.*

20

AFTER THE BREAKFAST, Veer retired to his study. He was in a pensive mood. Natasha was getting to him in ways that Amyra had never. He thought for a moment that he was having a panic attack in the morning when Dadi called Natasha over. She looked adorable, wrapped up in so much colourful wool. Her bohemian style of dressing was what made her quirky. His heart was beating so fast that he couldn't even greet her properly for fear of fumbling and embarrassing himself. *He was a bloody grown-up man; what was happening to him?* When his heartbeat normalized, he realized that Dadi was talking about some guy called Yayu and if he was the one. He was a little taken aback when Natasha declared that she loved him, but he gathered his wits swiftly and offered the car. He had wanted to walk with her to the foyer, but held back just in time. *She was a very young girl and he was a married man with a lot of problems... He better rein in his emotions. But why was he drawn so strongly to this girl? Was it because he was desperate to find somebody or was it because he had not felt so young and carefree like he did when he was with her, since his problems with Amyra began.*

Veer and Amyra had also had very good times; it wasn't always so bad. They were very good friends before they fell in love. Amyra was the prettiest girl in town with the brightest future; he was the outsider, struggler. Amyra cared for him and spoilt him with all her love. People used to be jealous at how much in sync they were. When they got married, they did a big spread for *Marie Claire* magazine and poured their hearts out for the world to know how much they loved each other. All was well and then he started becoming possessive and she, elusive. They were both very strong-headed and had big egos. Their friends tried to reason it out with them, tried to convince them that they must hold on to their love, but all good things come to an end and so did their relationship. The debacle left him bitter and in a lot of legal trouble. He never tried to sort things with her.

He had always been proud of his ability to compartmentalize the personal and the professional. Even during the most traumatic times with Amyra, Veer never lost sight of his work. He battled his emotions and put in more and more time at work. In fact, it was that very movie that earned him his first National Award. There was a huge uproar that a wife-beater had been awarded the prestigious National Award for Best Film, but the jury held its ground and there was a press release about how the allegations had still not been proven. Veer was elated at the prospect of being the youngest recipient of the National Award for Best Film and Best Direction. The media started hounding him again and then he shifted base to Landour-Mussorie. Mumbai had become too much for him. He picked up his plaque from its esteemed place at the showcase and looked at it very closely. *It was a very big achievement. He was an outsider in the film industry and had still been able to reach those heights. He must focus on his work.*

He sat down, determined to work on his pending script, when his phone rang. It was his lawyer. He was coming to Landour, and wanted to meet Veer. He sounded a little different than his usual calm self. Veer felt a little nervous. *What if he had bad news?*

'Yes, let's meet. Come over to my house directly,' Veer said.

With his mind all over the place, he couldn't work. So, he decided to pump up the music and hit the gym.

21

'ARE YOU SURE they have invited me? I mean *me*? Really? Oh my God! Wait till Shanaya hears. She drools over Veer and his looks,' he finally took a breath.

Natasha, like a mean friend, wanted to point out that his reaction to the invitation was over the top, but she held back. After the initial excitement and euphoria at being invited to Veer's house for dinner, Yayu became frantic with worry.

'What should I buy, Natasha? Tell me. I must take something for both of them,' Yayu asked for the fifth time.

'Yayu, just take some flowers for Dadi and a bottle of wine for Veer. Can we finish that already? You are driving me nuts.'

They had spent a perfect day sightseeing and lunching, this time at a South Indian restaurant. Towards the evening, Yayu started freaking out about the dinner again. Finally, after great deliberation, he decided on flowers and a not-very-expensive bottle of wine. Then he began his questions about how he looked. He wanted to change but Natasha put her foot down and refused. Throughout the drive up to the bungalow, Yayu kept pestering her for something or the other and she had to scream at him to stop his childish behaviour.

'Yayu, you have to calm down or I am dropping you back to your hotel. You can't embarrass me like this. In fact, you will embarrass yourself. Promise me that you will behave normally around Veer or I will turn back the car right away.'

Yayu gave a sheepish smile in affirmation.

At exactly 7 p.m., the car pulled in to the driveway. Natasha gave a look of reassurance to Yayu and stood in the foyer as he got down from the car. They were greeted by Lydia, who led them in and complimented them on being on time.

'Dadi is very punctual and she will really appreciate that you are on time,' said Lydia, as she signalled them to make themselves comfortable in the drawing room. 'I will inform Dadi that you are here.'

The setting of the drawing room looked a little different—*festive,* Natasha thought. Beautiful candles were lit at various places like on the mantle, on the corner tables and on the centre table. The light from the corner lamps added to the ambience. The incense infuser was making the whole area smell like a lavender farm. There were various little treats on a trolley parked next to the sofa. The bar cabinet looked fuller than usual and the glasses were already laid out. Ghazals were being played on the music system to set the mood. *Dadi had really gone out of her way for them.* Natasha felt both indebted and tense at the same time. *What was Veer thinking? Would he be nice to Yayu?*

She could only hope for the best.

Yayu was taking in the surroundings and the splendour of a Bollywood director's home, like a child in a candy store.

'Natasha, yaar, I knew these guys lived well, but I never imagined *this* well. It's grand and homey at the same time,' said Yayu, soaking in the luxurious setting.

Natasha smiled in agreement. Dadi chose the exact moment to make her entry. Lydia parked her wheelchair close to the sofas and not very far from the fireplace.

'Welcome, Yayu,' Dadi said, offering a handshake. Yayu got up promptly, took Dadi's hand and bent down a little in respect.

'Thank you, Dadi,' he said and then asked, 'Can I call you "Dadi"?'

Dadi smiled and replied, 'Of course, you can. I have become everyone's Dadi now,' she added with a wink. Both Yayu and Natasha laughed out loud.

The music from the chimes drew the attention of the group as Veer walked in from the rear end of the room. He had bumped into a wind chime and was rubbing his forehead.

'Ah, here he is,' said Dadi. It had been nearly half an hour since Dadi had been entertaining them. Veer's entry had a different effect on each of the three individuals waiting for his arrival: Dadi relaxed a bit, Yayu got up in respect and Natasha tensed up. Veer was wearing grey slacks, a black button-down shirt, a grey and black sweater and a pair of black suede loafers. *Casual, chic, stylish, classy—he was always so appropriately dressed.*

He walked up to Yayu and shook his hand. 'Welcome, Yayu. I hope Dadi is looking after you!' he said and then added, 'I am sorry for being late. I had some urgent business to attend to.'

Then he looked at Natasha. She had also gotten up as he had walked closer to Yayu. He came up to her, half-hugged her and sat next to her. She didn't hear him say 'hello'. She was so busy dealing with the effect his cologne and his body had had on her that she forgot to sit down. Yayu pulled her down. She dropped on to the sofa with a thud and glared at Yayu.

She loved Veer. Plain and simple—she loved him. Oh, he was so sexy, so manly and smelled delicious. Natasha wondered if people in the room could see her swooning. *Was he radiating heat? She could surely feel it.* Yayu laughed at something and that broke her reverie.

'What do you think, Natasha?' Dadi asked, trying to draw her in to the conversation. But Natasha had not been listening, so Yayu prompted her, 'We were talking about how beautiful the twin towns of Mussoorie and Landour are. What do you think?'

Natasha looked at him with gratitude for saving her ass and replied, 'Yes, yes, so much beauty. I had read about the beauty of Mussoorie in Ruskin Bond's books but to experience it is something else. Especially when I came here, the weather was so bad and it snowed so heavily that the town was at a standstill. Tragedy was about to strike Mussoorie like the rest of Uttarakhand, yet the beauty of the hill-town was surreal. I had never experienced snowfall and the smell of fresh snow on earth was as intoxicating as the smell of wet earth during the monsoons. I will never forget how it feels to touch the snow. You guys are really lucky you have a home here,' she finished off, looking at Dadi and then at Veer. He was listening to her intently and looking at her warmly. Natasha felt that warmth spread to her heart and to the pit of her stomach. *How will she get through this evening?*

During her testimony, the appetizers were brought in. It was a lavish spread that ranged from Italian bruschetta to Chinese spring rolls to Indian paneer tikka. There were various bowls of chips and crisps and masala dry fruits, along with multiple condiments. When Veer asked about drinks, Yayu hesitated in the presence of Dadi. But Dadi was very cool, 'Come on, don't mind me. It's very cold here. You must have the poison of your choice,' she put Yayu at ease and then ordered Veer, 'Natasha and I will have red wine, please.'

Yayu had been meaning to ask about Veer's journey in Bollywood and his craft but couldn't find an opening. Then, very kindly, Veer asked him what he did and what his future plans were. That's the opening Yayu had been looking for and he stepped in swiftly.

'Sir, I am doing the same course as Natasha in JNU. My interests are the same as her and I am having a bit of a fan moment here. Natasha had warned me that if I embarrass her, she will disown me,' he looked at Natasha, who shifted uncomfortably in her seat, her eyes pleading him to stop, 'but all I want is to ask you about your journey in Bollywood and about the art of direction. Please tell us,' Yayu looked at Veer hopefully.

Dadi egged Veer on, 'Yes, Veer, you must share your passion with these young kids. They are the future of the industry.' She looked affectionately at the young ones.

Veer shifted in his sofa, sipped on his drink and said, 'Ask away to your heart's delight.'

Yayu pounced on the opportunity to learn from the master. While the teacher and the tot were engaged in a serious conversation, ranging from camera angles, cameras, scripts, scriptwriters, adaptations and locations to producers and the thing that makes the world go around—money—Natasha was admiring the two men. Veer and Yayu were poles apart in terms of personality and physique. While Veer was tall, lanky and athletic, Yayu was the opposite—short, stocky and podgy. She had seen Veer work out in the gym; she knew what his body looked like. It was chiselled and perfect. She shifted uncomfortably as she remembered how broad his shoulders looked and how perfect his abs were. She had also seen Yayu numerous times in the swimming pool—he was round at the edges; never fat but not fit either. While Veer's clothes were immaculate and his hair was in place, Yayu's clothes were bohemian, with layers of various colours, and the hair was all over the place. Yayu was exactly like Natasha—impulsive, impatient, light-hearted, socially at ease and an extrovert. Veer was the exact opposite—serious, self-disciplined, hard worker with a passionate sense of aesthetics, and an introvert. Yayu was familiar, and kindled feelings of homey comfort, which one keeps wanting to go back to, again and again. Veer, on the other hand, ignited passion in her, filled her heart with love, and her body with lust. She wanted to own him, be him, inside him, outside him. She wanted to jump him and take him till she felt satisfied, and then lie next to him, spent. She had never been intimate with anyone, other than a kiss here and there. She had never wanted to. But with Veer, things were different. She saw as Veer ran his hand through his hair; her heart sang. *He was perfect. Why was he acting so weird? Does he not feel anything that I feel?* She was sliding into depression when Dadi called her name.

'Yes, Dadi?' she asked, then she looked around and saw that the dinner had been laid and Dadi was asking her to start. Everyone was looking at her. She blushed a little and then sheepishly picked up a dinner plate. Dadi was explaining how she preferred to have food laid out here in the drawing room, instead of the dining room because they were a small group and she liked informality. Everybody agreed with her.

During dinner, the conversation veered towards Natasha and Yayu's friendship. Dadi wanted to know how they became friends and if they had known each other long. Yayu was eager to talk about his girlfriend as well. When he was talking about Shanaya, Natasha felt anxious but Veer looked surprisingly calm. She had wanted to give Veer the impression that Yayu was very special to her, to see if he got jealous, but Yayu spilled the beans on Shanaya and spoilt her plans. She just wanted the dinner to be over now.

As they stood up to leave, Dadi asked Lydia to bring a packet. It was a neatly wrapped gift for Yayu.

'I want you to have this and feel free to come over whenever you want. This is your home, Yayu. And being surrounded by young people also makes me feel young.' She patted his back as he bent down to hug her. Ram Singh was asked to drop Yayu back to his hotel and the moment his car left, Natasha thanked Dadi for being so kind and excused herself on the pretext of being exhausted. She had just about closed the door to her room, when someone knocked. *Was it Veer?* She thought she had heard Veer call her name, but wasn't sure. *What did he want now?*

22

VEER HAD BEEN dreading the dinner. With all that was happening with his lawyer, he had just wanted to shut himself up in his room and not talk to anyone. Dadi's dinner plans clashed with his plans for solitude. He had also wanted to get to know who Yayu was and why he was so special to Natasha. Strangely, he felt jealous when Natasha was talking about Yayu. He liked how her eyes lit up every time she mentioned home or Nani or Yayu. It meant that she came from a happy family and probably that was where her confidence came from—the fact that somebody always had her back. Veer knew the feeling; he had always felt like that till his parents had passed away. His relatives were very supportive and Dadi was always around, but somehow he could never be that trusting again.

He was lost in some thought when the wind chime had hit him. He had felt so stupid at making a fool of himself, in his own house. When he looked up, he saw two kids wrapped up in colourful sweaters and mufflers sitting next to Dadi. *These guys were really young,* he thought to himself and they looked similar to each other too. During the course of the night, it was established that Natasha and Yayu were just friends but the way they completed each other's sentences or looked at each other with such affection, there was much more to their friendship than they realized. There were friendships and then there was *the* friendship. Yayu and Natasha had a friendship that would last a lifetime. No man or woman would be able to break it because the basis of their relationship was respect and understanding. He was extremely jealous of their bond.

Veer had chosen to sit next to Natasha because he wanted to be close to her. That her scent would play havoc with his senses was something he was not prepared for. He knew he should be careful and not act like a sixteen-year-old lovelorn teenager. *Lovelorn? Love? Was he in love? No, he wasn't, and he wouldn't even think about it. Natasha had come to him to learn the art of movie-making, to be his intern, and here he was, sulking after her and losing focus.* While he was discussing direction and scriptwriting with Yayu, he had realized that he had not really focused on Natasha's learning. He had given her a task and hadn't even asked if she had finished it. *He should be able to mentor a young person more professionally.* It was then that he decided to talk to Natasha about her work before the night ended.

23

WITH A HEARTBEAT like the drumbeat of a rock band, Natasha opened the door. It was Lydia. She was disappointed and relieved at the same time.

'What is it, Lydia?' asked Natasha.

'Ma'am, Sir is asking for you. He wants you to join him in the study,' Lydia replied and handed her the day's newspaper.

Natasha's interest was piqued. She looked at the time. It was half past 11. Not too late by Delhi standards, but in Mussoorie, it was literally the middle of the night. *Why should Veer call her at this hour in the study?*

Without wasting any time, she pulled on her jacket, which she had carelessly thrown on the bed, and followed Lydia. She felt nervous and excited at the same time. She had not been alone with Veer since that night. *What will he do now when they would be alone?* She had expected him to at least talk about what happened the other night, but she was too proud to mention it if he had decided to steer clear of the conversation. She noticed that her palms were a little sweaty as she knocked on the door of the study.

'Come in,' a guttural, manly voice called her in. The room was amply lit but the view from the French windows looked a little scary at night. Twinkling lights were strewn across the clear skies and the majestic mountains looked daunting. Veer was sitting at his table with a laptop open and various papers strewn across the table. He looked edgy, serious and fastidious, with a pen in his hand and a pair of spectacles resting on the bridge of his nose. *How can someone look geeky and sexy at the same time?* She noticed that he had pulled back the sleeves of his shirt and sweater together and that gave him a rugged, sensual look. 'Come, Natasha, have a seat.'

Natasha sat down uneasily. She realized that this was not about her girly romantic escapades. Veer meant business. She took out her phone from her pocket and kept it on vibration mode. She wished that she had carried her laptop.

'Natasha, I have not been able to guide you as I would have liked to,' he looked at her, 'I mean to correct that lapse. You are here to learn about filmmaking and I intend to teach you,' he added, determined. 'I had asked you to work on Nora's characterization and adaptation in the Indian scenario. I assessed the paper that you had kept here. You have done a great job. You have been taught well. I really liked that bit you added about the red lipstick and how that's the only makeup she wears and it lifts her up always. Following that, I want you to watch Mike Newell's *Mona Lisa Smile*.' Handing her the DVD, he added, 'Critically, this time. I want you look at it as a filmmaker. Divide the film into three parts: pre-production, filming and post-production. You must make a list of things you feel the director must have done in all the three stages. Tell me what you could have done differently. Make notes on cinematography, lighting, camera … Any questions?' Veer could be ruthless when it came to compartmentalization. Natasha was a novice at all that. She was still wondering if he would mention the kiss.

'Don't you have anything else to say to me?' Natasha challenged him.

Veer took the bait, 'I don't want to complicate our professional relationship. Let's focus on work for now.'

How could she have given him the power to hurt her so much?

'Yes, we must be professional, but don't you think it is already complicated?' Natasha got up from her chair and went to the French window. She was feeling very emotional and she didn't want him to see that.

Now, it was Veer's turn to feel confused.

What was happening here? Was she going to cry? Oh God! He couldn't deal with tears.

He went to her but maintained a distance. Natasha's hair was dishevelled and her clothes were unruly, but her smell was intoxicating. She smelled of flowers and rain and it was driving Veer crazy. She was still looking out of the window, seemingly lost in thought when he reached out to caress her hair. He didn't realize that he had actually reached out and touched it, till she reacted. She turned around and found him standing right behind her. Her instinct was to go forward and hug him, but she didn't know how he would react. He was so tall that Natasha's eyes just about reached his torso. That meant she couldn't look him in the eye. When she looked up, she saw that he was looking down at her. There was pain, confusion and a hint of desire in his eyes. It took Natasha's breath away.

'So, when shall I meet you with my inputs?' Natasha asked, getting away from him.

Coming back to his desk, Veer replied, 'Tomorrow evening would be best. That would give you enough time to prepare. So, 5 p.m. sharp in my study.'

Natasha nodded and hurried out of the room. Veer flopped down on his chair with a thud. He would have kissed her again had she not moved away. He really wanted to. When she had turned around, her beauty had devastated him. Her eyes were glistening, moist on the edges, flawless skin, full pink lips, arched eyebrows, and a sharp nose that was a little red on the tip. As a director, he had worked with the most beautiful faces of Bollywood, but there was something innocent about this girl that was driving him mad and making him lose control. He had unknowingly scribbled something on the writing pad kept under his hand when Natasha had gone up to the window.

Tumhare gham ki dali uthakar
Zubaan pe rakh li hai dekho maine
Ye qatra qatra pighal rahi hai,
Main qatra qatra hi jee raha hun

Gulzar's popular ghazal sung by Jagjit Singh was playing in his mind. He felt that the description in the couplet was clearly the description of his situation. He did feel that he was living with pain, but was it because of Natasha or Amyra? Was he sad about Amyra? He was drawn towards Natasha but he was not a hundred per cent sure that he could act on it. He wanted to, but he had to be surer than he was.

24

NATASHA WAS STANDING next to the French window in the study, looking at the majestic mountains and the twinkling lights. It was past midnight. The silence of the night was broken only by the calls of a cricket here or there. The big house was very quiet, alive only with the breathing sounds of Natasha and Veer. When she turned around, he was standing just behind her, his eyes full of love and desire. She came forward and hugged him. He tilted her face up to kiss her. A brush on the lips to begin with but increasing in intensity as his tongue looked to possess her. An involuntary moan escaped from her mouth. Her hands reached up to hold on to his shoulders as the onslaught of his kiss increased. He anchored her with one hand under her head and the other on the small of her back. Their breathing was becoming more ragged as desire and hunger for each other exploded. When it was too much to stand, Veer carefully led her to the couch near the fireplace. He sat down and made her sit on his lap. Engulfed in his arms, she was floating in a mixture of heat, sex and desire. She wanted more and had proof that he also wanted to move forward. He was now kissing her neck, while taking off her jacket. She had thrown her head back to give him access to more. Once the jacket hit the floor, Veer's hands were seeking inside the T-shirt. Carefully staying clear of her breasts and running up and down her spine, on her stomach, near her navel, near the band of her jeans, probing just a little but not going further. She wanted more, wanted him to touch her more. She pressed herself to him, asking for more. It was like he had read her mind and

Buzz … Buzz … Buzz …

Buzz … Buzz … Buzz …

What is vibrating? Is that her phone? Natasha looked for it under her pillow. Nani was calling her. It was 11 in the morning and she was dreaming about making out with Veer. She woke up, angry and frustrated. She told Nani that she would call her back in a while, before cutting the call abruptly. She put her face on the pillow and screamed into it to vent her frustration. She had to get a grip on herself. She looked for the DVD of *Mona Lisa Smile* and grabbed a writing pad, her headphones and the laptop. She put everything on the small table next to the French window overlooking the front lawn. She was determined to not let the dream spoil her day. *She will work hard. This was her career and she better make the best of this opportunity to work with the best in the business.*

∽

As the credits of the picture rolled, Natasha looked down at her notes. She had spent the last five hours on a movie she had already watched thrice. This time when she watched it, she was not only following the plot and admiring the beauty of the female leads and wishing that she was there, she was also carefully observing the camera angles, the setting of the stage, and the crests and troughs in the scriptwriting. It was a movie about a teacher who taught the history of art—portrayed by Julia Roberts, in the 1950s post-World War II era—who encouraged and inspired young women of a private liberal arts college to pursue their individuality. She shows them the difference between the roles that society defines for them traditionally and the roles that they could choose for themselves. She also read various reviews of the movie and downloaded the 'Behind the Scenes with the Director' video to better equip herself for her tête-à-tête with Veer in the evening. She wanted to dazzle him with her preparation and her looks. Natasha smiled at her reflection in the now black screen of the laptop.

For the next few hours till her meeting with Veer, Natasha caught up with Nani and Yayu. She also spoke to one of her professors, who had written to her about the progress in her internship with Gazaffar. Professor Siddharth Singla was one of the youngest professors of the department. He looked out for Natasha and knew that she really wanted to be a filmmaker. He was 'only' shocked to hear about what happened to her internship with Gazaffar and thrilled to hear about her chance internship with Veer Singh Tomar. He told her to be focused and learn from the young director. He told her to ask him as many questions as she can and reminded her that no question was a stupid question when the aim was to learn. He sensed some tension in her voice and asked her about it. She lied about the real reason for her melancholia and told him that she was tense about presenting her thoughts to Veer about the movie assignment. He told her to be herself, and that he had confidence in her abilities and her training, referring to her teachers at the Arts and Aesthetics School at JNU. Last but not the least, he told her to 'not fall in love with the young, bad boy of Bollywood' and she didn't have the heart to tell him that it was too late for that. She had not only fallen in love with him, she was very sure he was aware that she had fallen in love with him. *Could he suggest a remedy? Could anyone suggest a course of recovery?*

25

'*AAH KO CHAHIYE ek umr asar hone tak,*' Veer said out loud as she entered the study. It was 5 in the evening and it was already dark in Mussoorie. 'Do you think Ghalib was really in love when he wrote that?' Veer looked intensely at Natasha. She had decided to dazzle but not be dazzled. She looked stunning in an indigo Fabindia kurta and white palazzo pants. She had worn a khadi silk Nehru jacket and brought a shawl along, just in case it became colder. In typical JNU style, she was wearing colourful socks with Reebok sandals and a file folder from Dilli Haat completed her look. She was wearing her hair down, parted in the middle, a black bindi donned her forehead and thick kohl lined her eyes. The beautiful silver jhumkis that she had forcefully taken from Nani, twinkled on her ears. She knew that it had the desired effect when Veer tried helplessly to look away from her and got caught sneaking a peek.

She pulled a chair opposite him and replied, '*Kaun jeeta hai teri zulf ke sar hone tak*. Incidently, this is Yayu's favourite couplet too. He has recited Urdu sher-o-shayari to me since forever. I think he means to convey the message the couplet carries, but I always take it for its literary value. He is very theatrical as such.'

Veer was hit with something raw in his gut. There was such affection in her eyes when she talked about Yayu. Such nonchalance. Such confidence. He admired that about her. She was a loyal friend. He could tell that she would go to any lengths to help Yayu. He needed that in his life. All his so-called loyal friends had parted ways with him when Amyra had left him. Some of them had tried to be pally again when he had won the National Award, but he had matured by then and could see through them.

Natasha's eyes had wavered to his lips. Soft. Brown. Smoker's lips. She wanted him to kiss her. She remembered his taste from that night. It was a mix of wine and chocolate. *Does he want to kiss me? Would he ever again?*

Veer was looking at her eyes. Such expressive, big, beautiful eyes. The bindi on her forehead added to her sex appeal. She was dressed to kill. *This girl was something else.* All he wanted was to take her in his arms and never let her go. Instead, he asked, 'So, do you think Ghalib was in love or not?'

'He couldn't have not been,' she replied, bringing her attention back to him. 'For anyone to have such poignant thoughts, it has to be love. Whether it was love for God, love for a girl, love for his wife, or love for the self, that needs to be seen. But love is what makes the world go around, or let me put it this way, Ghalib was definitely in love when he wrote that.'

Out of the blue, he asked, 'What do you do when you are in love?' He regretted it the moment it came out of his mouth.

Natasha looked surprised. She smiled and answered, 'I hide.'

She then opened her folder. She was not going to talk about that with him. She would give herself away and there still was a long way to go if she wanted something fruitful from this whole exercise.

'I watched the movie. I am ready with my notes. Shall we start?'

Veer was very professional, but Natasha was ruthlessly so. He could see so much of his young self in her. The same determination, the same drive. *He should not put her in a spot like that.* He made a mental note of that and asked, 'So, what did you think about the script?' Over the next hour, Natasha elaborated all her learnings from the film and critiqued various issues. She also highlighted some production concerns and listed out all the planning done in the pre, post and filming stage. Veer was amazed at her insights on lighting and camera angles. *She was not just a beautiful face. She meant business. She knew her subject and was eager to learn. She was the perfect student and could be his perfect protégé if he handled this carefully.* The filmmaker in him got excited at the prospect of imparting knowledge to a smart student, but he hid his glee.

'Good. You have great insights into the art of filmmaking. I am very happy with your work and would like you to continue working with me on the new film that I am working on. But now, let us work on an Indian filmmaker to understand how Indian minds work. Do you want to choose someone?' he asked her, giving her an opportunity to choose the direction her life would take. Her choice of filmmaker would tell him a lot about her. It would also decide if he would continue working with her in the future. 'Though I would want you to choose someone you have not worked on during your course,' he added the caveat, because he remembered the extensive course papers of the department that they were both the alumnus of.

'I worked extensively on Satyajit Ray for my course, so he is out. I always wanted to work on Guru Dutt. Do you think I could work on that?' she hesitated a bit, but that was exactly what he wanted.

'You could not have chosen better,' he confirmed.

He got up and walked towards his extensive library. Natasha followed him. He reached up and took out two books on Guru Dutt—*Guru Dutt: A life less lived* and *Guru Dutt: A Tragedy*. She had already read the first one and owned a copy signed by the author. She had also gone to the book-reading session by the author at the India Habitat Centre. She didn't tell Veer this, though. She took both the books and the Blu-ray DVDs of Guru Dutt's movies from him. Their hands touched and electricity buzzed between them. Both of them looked up at the same moment. Their eyes locked. They wanted more. Much more. He could feel her pulse where his fingers supported her hand to take the load off his hands. Her breath quickened. *How would she react if he threw caution to the winds and kissed her now? That would complicate life. Life was not as lovely as the first kiss on a drunken night. He knew better than most.* He let go.

'I would like to discuss your progress on this, the day after, as I have a meeting tomorrow.'

She nodded and left the room as quickly as she could, adjusting the pile of books and DVDs on top of her folder.

26

Main doon bhi to kya doon tumhe aye shokh nazaaro
Le de ke mere paas kuch aansu hai, kuch aahe...

GURU DUTT LIT up the screen as the quintessential struggler of the post-Independence era, in the movie *Pyaasa*. Natasha had watched the movie several times, with Yayu and alone. The depth of the movie was never lost on her. Written by Abrar Alvi, and directed and produced by, and starring, Guru Dutt, it was one of the greatest movies of all time, beautifully interspersed with the nazms of Sahir Ludhianvi brought to life by S.D. Burman's music. Hemant Kumar's rendition of '*Bichhad gayaa har saathi dekar pal do pal ka saath; Kisko fursat hai jo thaame deewanon ka haath; Humko apna saaya tak, aqsar bezaar mila*' always filled her heart with pain and anguish. The mood of the movie reverberated with her feelings. She welled up at Vijay's (Guru Dutt) question to Gulab (Waheeda Rehman), '*To phir main yahan kya kar raha hun? Main kyon zinda hun, Gulab?*' She had thought of the same thing numerous times when she was under the weather, but she always picked herself up and repeated to herself, 'When life gives you lemons, make lemonade.'

Each of Guru Dutt's movies was so thought-provoking that she needed some time to recuperate before starting the next. Natasha had been watching the movies since morning and not left the room after coming back from the study last night, skipping breakfast completely. She was certain that Veer had seen her leaning in for the kiss just before he let go abruptly. She came back to the room all worked up. *She would not let herself get distracted,* she had made up her mind before she had gone to meet Veer, but the moment he was close to her, she'd lost all reason.

Lydia had called her for lunch thirty minutes back and while going down, Natasha was sure that Veer would have eaten by then. She wanted to avoid meeting him if she could. She could hear sweet, joyful laughter coming from the dining room. Infectious laughter. The kind that would echo in each room and all corners of the house and make everyone happy. A beautiful girl, in her early twenties, was sitting at the table with Veer. She looked divine in her red wool dress and flowing hair. Her dress ended just above the knees and her stockinged legs looked perfect. She was sitting next to Veer and not across him. Her manicured fingers were on Veer's wrist as he talked about something, which she found particularly funny and threw her head back in laughter. Her lips were a luscious red and drew attention. She saw Veer lean in as the lady in red whispered something in his ear. Veer laughed. Pure laughter. Laughter that shook the body and affected the soul. For a moment, Natasha was dumbstruck. She had not seen Veer like this in the last few days that she had stayed here. The lady went ahead and put her arm on his shoulder to bring him closer. Natasha was tempted to run back to her room and let them be, but Lydia called her out at that very moment. Veer turned around to find Natasha standing near the door. His face became stoic and his serious demeanour returned. *That was the Veer she knew.*

'Come, Natasha,' Veer gestured her over. He stood up as she joined them. 'Natasha, meet Riya. She is a model, enjoys cricket and loves to prank people,' Veer said, introducing Riya.

'I pranked you once, Veer, *once*,' Riya said in protest. Veer hugged her in return.

'Riya and I have been friends for a long time,' Veer added.

They had chemistry. Natasha recognized her from the various magazines spreads and fashion weeks. Riya was not *a* model, she was *the* model. She was the reigning queen of the modelling world.

'Riya meet Natasha. Natasha is about to graduate from the School of Arts and Aesthetics in JNU and is going to be a filmmaker. She is interning with me, helping me with the movie that you are going to star in,' Veer gave a gentle nudge to Riya, who brought her hand forward to shake Natasha's.

'Natasha, you are very lucky to be interning with Veer. A million budding filmmakers would give their right hands to be where you are.'

Was there a hint of envy in Riya's statement? But she didn't have to be jealous. She was a famous model and had Veer eating out of her hand. Literally.

Riya was forcing Veer to have some Greek yoghurt that she had brought along. Natasha developed an instant dislike for Riya. She had lost her appetite for the afternoon and had probably developed intolerance for Greek yoghurt for the rest of her life. She tried to eat something to be polite and was done in a jiffy. She didn't want to hang around even a moment longer than necessary. She got up to leave, but Veer told her to be ready by 7 in the evening for a party that some of his friends were throwing in Riya's honour.

Natasha's first thought was that she didn't have anything to wear but then she calmed down and reminded herself that she should be exactly who she is, and be proud of it. Very graciously, she excused herself and ran up to her room the moment she was out of sight of Veer. She was a little perplexed with Riya. Natasha had not anticipated that jealousy will strike with such strength as it did when she saw the easy chemistry between Riya and Veer. *Some girls had it all—beauty, grace, a good figure, and to top it off, luck!* She didn't want to know what was going on between them. She hardened herself to the fact that Veer was an adult and has many friends and girlfriends. Instead of focusing on her moping heart, she decided to focus on the party that evening.

This would be her maiden entry into the Bollywood party scene and that was happening much before she had anticipated, even before her formal entry into the Indian film industry. She decided that she had to be herself and not seek appreciation or try to belong. She had brought her favourite saris and dresses, keeping Gazaffar's choices in mind. She knew there would be parties and she didn't want to go unprepared lest she got invited. She chose an emerald green Fabindia sari in khadi silk and a cream silk blouse, with Nani's pashmina and her polki and silver jewellery. Thick kohl gave further depth to her eyes. She chose to wear a pink lip colour, which gave her face a softness in contrast to her dark eye makeup. Her hair was tied in a loose messy bun. A few drops of Clinique Happy, which she had begged Nani to buy for her, set the mood for the evening. She knew she was looking beautiful and *herself*.

Riya had gone ahead as she wanted to dress up for the party and her bags were at the hotel. Veer was waiting for Natasha in the foyer and turned around at the 'tic-tac' of her heels. She looked smashing and it was difficult for him to not react to it. Veer opened the door for her and she sat down carefully, adjusting her pallu.

After five minutes into the drive when Veer had still not spoken, Natasha dared.

'What are you thinking?'

Veer couldn't have told her that for the past five minutes, he was contemplating whether to compliment her or not, so he said, 'Nothing in particular…I am a little apprehensive of facing a crowd. This is the first time since my separation with Amyra that I would be meeting all of them together. I have met some of them individually, but not all together. Even when I won the National Award, they had wanted to throw a party for me but I stopped them; I wasn't ready. But today, when Riya came and asked me to come, I decided to make the effort.'

Natasha had not expected such an honest answer from Veer. She took her time and then said, 'It will be okay, Veer. They are, after all, your friends. Just be yourself and the evening shall pass,' she put her hand on his hand, to comfort him. Veer pulled up the car on the side of the road and looked at her. Such beautiful eyes filled with hope, the innocence of youth, the intoxicating smell of Natasha—all became too overwhelming.

…He turned around, leaned and claimed her lips. At first, he registered shock in her reaction and as he became insistent, she responded. He nipped on her bottom lip and she moaned. She was now straining against the seat belt to lean in to him. He released the seat belt with one hand and caressed her back with the other. His hand on the skin of her back, sent shivers down her spine. Her hand was on his ear and was gently stroking him…

The loud horn of a car coming from behind brought him back to reality. He was still in his seat, not kissing Natasha, and she was asking him, 'Are you okay, Veer?'

He had actually hallucinated the whole kiss. That was how

much he wanted to kiss her. He stepped out of the car and lit a cigarette. Surprisingly, he did not feel guilty at the prospect of kissing her at all. *In fact, it felt so right this time.*

Natasha opened the door of the car to join him on the road, but Veer said, 'Don't come out, I am coming in. It's too cold outside.' He threw away the cigarette butt and joined her in the car. Veer wanted to know if she was okay.

In return, she asked, 'Do I look okay?' pointing at her face.

Veer smiled at her and said, 'Ravishing,' and started the engine.

Natasha touched up her makeup on the way. They reached their destination in less than ten minutes, but those ten minutes were one of the most exciting ten minutes of her life. She felt happy and thrilled and hopeful and ecstatic. Happy music played and filled their hearts with the song of life. During that ten-minute journey, he looked at her with affection and desire in his eyes. His eyes held promise for more later that night.

27

'I THINK THIS is the place,' Veer said, looking at the address in the message on his phone. The place was an old bungalow from the British times, that his friends claimed to have hired in the message. It was completely quiet; he walked in with Natasha's hand in his. As he pushed open the front door, people screamed 'Surprise!' and rushed out to them from their hiding places from behind the curtains and turned on all the lights. A big banner congratulating Veer for his success was hung up in the middle of the room. There were more than thirty men and women immaculately dressed in western casuals. Natasha was still standing at the door and Veer was already lost in the crowd. He was surrounded by screaming, shouting, excited people, but Natasha's eyes were drawn to one woman in particular, who had her back to her. She was dressed in a designer black dress—an LBD, to be specific—had a figure to kill for and was holding back from the crowd. It wasn't Riya; she could see her jumping up and down with other models. *Who was she?*

Then the crowd parted and released Veer. And the look on his face told her who she was.

It was Amyra.

Veer saw Amyra and froze. *What was she doing here? Was this her plan? This must be her plan! Oh God. How could he be so naïve? Of course, she had planned this!*

She came forward to meet him and he couldn't but be polite. They hugged like old friends who had fought and were finding it difficult to reconnect. As he hugged her reluctantly, he saw Natasha still standing at the door, looking at him. He knew he was in deeper shit than he had been when this day had begun.

Veer walked up to Natasha.

'Everybody, meet Natasha. She is interning with me,' Veer put his hand on her shoulder and declared to the crowd. The crowd cheered, 'Hi Natasha!' and then everybody went about their business of drinking and dancing.

The 1990s' party music, drinks and food made the party bubble with excitement. Natasha had expected a more sophisticated party and was surprised that *these* people partied like young college kids. Amyra followed Veer to meet Natasha. She was more beautiful than her pictures. The camera didn't do her justice. She was exquisite. Natasha was suddenly feeling foolish and out of place in a sari when she was surrounded by the lissom beauties of the Indian fashion circuit.

'Hello Natasha; Amyra,' she said, introducing herself.

'Hello Amyraji, of course I know you. It's a pleasure meeting you,' replied Natasha.

Veer was extremely angry at being played like that. Amyra had made various attempts to reach Veer in the last few days since the Uttarkashi cloudburst disaster. She had called at home numerous times and Veer had specifically instructed Lydia to not tell her where he was. She had also tried to contact him through his lawyer, but he turned her down every time. She had written emails to him, sent messages to him—all to no avail. Veer was not interested in any dialogue with her. He wanted a divorce. She had also wanted a divorce, but his winning the National Award had changed her mind. She had first sent feelers, then friends, and had finally come herself.

Veer was sitting in a corner, sulking, with a drink in his hand and Amyra glued to his side. The rest of the gang had left them alone, to catch up. Veer saw that Natasha was surrounded by a young crowd. He could identify two young models and two young men, who were probably ADs. Natasha was shining amongst them. She was so full of life and energy and looked amazing. He loved how she tucked a few tendrils that had come loose, behind her ears. The ADs looked like they had already fallen in love with the earthy beauty. She stood out in the crowd. Engulfed in six yards of emerald green silk and a cream pashmina, her figure was still peeking out of it in the most exciting ways. Her perfect waist made him want to run his fingers up and down it till she moaned. *What the hell was he thinking? He must get a grip.* He got up to get a drink, without realizing that Amyra was saying something. He walked up to the group that surrounded Natasha.

'Hey guys, I hope you are not troubling my young friend,' he said, referring to Natasha.

'No Sir, we are not. In fact, we have found that we have many common friends and were connecting over our various favourite hangout places in Delhi,' said Ishaan.

Ishaan had worked with Veer in his last movie. He was a very bright guy and girls were drawn to him like a moth to a flame, but he could see that Ishaan was taken with Natasha. *He didn't like that. But what could he do?*

'Make sure that Natasha has fun,' he told Ishaan and went to sit with Riya.

The next two hours felt like a lifetime to Veer. He dodged every attempt Amyra made to talk to him. When she confronted him, he walked away. Finally, he told Riya to inform Amyra to meet him at Marriott for coffee at 5 in the evening, the day after. And then he was so drained that he decided to have a few more drinks quickly and dance like crazy. That was so out of character for him that some people held back and stared at him, but then everyone joined him on the floor with the music pumping high and the room lit up by only a few candles.

Natasha had seen what was happening with Amyra. She had felt a little insecure, hopeless and unhappy when she had first realized Amyra had thrown this party for Veer. With the kind of tension that surrounded them, even a blind person would be able to make out what was going on. Amyra was making an attempt to win Veer back, and he was resisting it. She knew it couldn't have happened all of a sudden. She must have been trying for a while to have finally come to this, and that is when the realization finally hit her that Veer was a married man. He was still legally wedded to Amyra and she was way too young to realize the nuances of a marriage gone wrong. This was also the moment when she realized that she must put her heart and soul into this party, have fun, make friends and network, which will help her in her career. It was then that she started mingling with the young crowd. She instantly gelled with Ishaan and realized that they had some common friends. When Veer started dancing, she was a little surprised but Ishaan didn't waste a second and led her to the floor. With a few drinks lifting up her spirits, Natasha danced like there was no tomorrow.

Veer saw her dancing with Ishaan, and then leading her outside the room by the hand. He followed them outside but stopped just a few metres away when he realized that Ishaan was kissing

Natasha. One of his arms was around her head to cradle it and the other was on her exposed waist. Natasha didn't seem to mind. Veer's instinct was to rip Ishaan away from Natasha and slap him, but he didn't do anything. He just went inside and turned off the music. Then somebody went outside to call Ishaan and Natasha. Everybody was a little tipsy by then and didn't really mind when Veer decided to call it a night. He asked Natasha if she wanted to come with him and she nodded.

'I hope you are not driving?' Natasha asked.

'No, I am not. Ram Singh is here to pick us up,' Veer replied, as they walked out of the party amidst cheering, screaming, drunk people waving goodbye.

During the journey back home, Natasha was fast asleep on Veer's shoulder and he was leaning into her. When Ram Singh called them, they woke up with a start. Natasha got out of the car quickly, and Veer followed her.

He called out to her, 'Natasha, I hope you had a nice time.' He was completely drunk.

'Yes, Sir, I did,' she replied. She was a little tipsy but quite sober.

'Sir?' he questioned.

'At the party, I realized that everybody calls you "sir" and I should too, so, "sir" it is from now on,' she beamed, a little too happy.

'Oh, really? But I guess we are way past those formalities, Natasha. I would like you to call me by my given name. Also, I hope you are working on your assignment…come to the study at 11 a.m. for a discussion,' he made a move to go forward and she turned at the same time.

They bumped into each other and she lost her balance. He

lunged forward to support her and his hands held on to her exposed waist. Their eyes locked into each other; they were very close to each other. She could hear him breathe, and he could hear her heart racing. She was sure that her skin had burnt where his warm hands had held her. Her eyes were pools of desire and longing. But that angered him.

'Do you like Ishaan?' Veer looked directly into her eyes.

Desire was replaced by confusion and then understanding, as she realized that he must have seen them outside on the porch. She opened her mouth to refute what he was thinking, to tell him that she had immediately pushed him away, that she had been polite to Ishaan because he was a nice boy and was a little drunk, and that he immediately realized that she didn't want it. That there was no kiss! That she didn't 'like' Ishaan.

But he didn't give her an opportunity. He just said, 'Don't bother,' and walked away.

28

AFTER FITFULLY TWISTING and turning on her bed for nearly an hour and going over everything that had transpired in the party and after, again and again, Natasha gave up. She was not going to be able to sleep and it was anyway close to daybreak, so she decided to watch another Guru Dutt movie 'critically'.

She had not watched *Sahib Bibi Aur Ghulam*, but like millions of Indians, she had been serenaded by an intoxicated Meena Kumari singing, '*Na jao saiyyan chhuda ke baiyyan, kasam tumhari main ro padungi.*' The story revolved around the system of zamindars and havelis and how the 'chhoti bahu', played by Meena Kumari, becomes a desperate alcoholic in her attempt to win back her husband. Bhootnath, played by Guru Dutt, is smitten by her beauty and becomes close to her. The main controversy surrounding the movie was about the direction. While Abrar Alvi claimed to be the director of the film, the style was so similar to Guru Dutt's, that it was very difficult to believe that it wasn't the latter's. While watching the movie, Natasha fell asleep, oblivious to the world. The movie ended, the laptop's battery discharged and the room was engulfed in darkness but for the orangish light from the mosquito repellent machine. She didn't dream that night or in the early morning. She had wanted to explain to Veer that he had misunderstood her dealings with regard to Ishaan, but when he didn't give her a chance, she became cool about it. She didn't think she owed anyone any explanation about kissing or not kissing a particular guy, especially not Veer.

~

Veer had called her to the study at 11 in the morning and she had set the alarm for 10 a.m. to give herself enough time to prepare as well as get ready, but what eventually happened was something that happened a lot to people like Natasha—people who completely rely on mobile phones for everything. She depended on her phone to remind her to have water, to wish her Nani for her birthday, to fill up various forms, to top-up her phone's balance, and to wake her up in the morning. In all the anger of the 'Ishaan fiasco' and the excitement of the filmy party, Natasha had forgotten to charge her phone and the battery had died. When Natasha didn't turn up by quarter past 11, Veer sent Lydia to her room.

Natasha awoke at the loud banging on the door. She ran towards it and found Lydia standing on the other side.

'What happened?' Natasha was furious.

'Ma'am, Sir has been waiting for you in the study. He asked me to remind you for your meeting at 11. It's now twenty minutes past 11.' Lydia pointed at her wristwatch and asked Natasha to hurry up.

Natasha had never been late for any of her meetings; Nani had instilled the value of punctuality in her since childhood. She ran helter-skelter to reach as early as possible, but became very nervous when she realized that she was not alone. Riya and Ishaan had joined them for the discussion, along with Veer. Both Riya and Ishaan still looked stoned and jaded. Ishaan had said 'hello' to her from under his sunglasses. Veer glared at her as Natasha took the seat opposite to him.

'As you all know, I am working on a new project that is based on Henrik Ibsen's play, *A Doll's House*. It was a path-breaking script when it had been staged in the nineteenth century. The essence of the play is not about feminism; it's about human excellence and human freedom. It's about one's right as a human being to experience all aspects of life and then choose for oneself, with nothing holding them back. When Nora closes that door, I don't want the audience to feel her ire, her emotions, her sentiments and sympathize with her; I want the audience to understand that equality and freedom are the rights of a human being, irrespective of their being a man or a woman.' Veer nervously ran his hand through his hair. Riya, Ishaan and Natasha were listening carefully.

'We will start working on the project immediately. Natasha will assist me with the writing part; Ishaan has already AD'd for me once, so he knows what I expect of him, in terms of pre-production, the searching of locales and tying up loose ends before filming begins. The catch in all this is that the producers want Amyra to star in the movie and only on that condition will it go on floor.'

There was pin-drop silence.

Veer carried on, 'You all know that our relationship is not very amicable right now, but we have to get past that. I am meeting her in the evening to figure out how to go about it. Now, Riya, I hope you will agree to play the second lead in my Indianized version of *A Doll's House*?'

Riya agreed instantly. She had been waiting to work with Veer for a while now. So, it was like a dream come true when he asked her to play the second lead.

'Also,' Veer looked at Riya with nearly an appeal, 'you will have to keep Amyra calm. I know she listens to you, and this movie is my dream project, so I was hoping you would help me sort that out.' Riya grinned in return and that was all Veer needed.

'On that note, the two of you can go and sleep. I know you are cursing me,' Veer said, looking at Riya and Ishaan, who had partied till the wee hours of the morning and were really not in the mood to get up when Veer had called them and asked them to come over (but who in his right mind, and at the beginning of his career, would say no to Veer!) So, they came, but all they really wanted was to curl up under a thick blanket and sleep. Veer and Natasha followed Riya and Ishaan to the foyer, where Ram Singh was waiting for them.

As the car went out of the driveway and took a left turn, Natasha turned and started walking inside. Veer called her name. One is usually very attached to one's name, and if that name is uttered by someone who you wish will call you again and again, it's even more intimate. Veer walked up to her.

'Care for a walk?' he asked.

'Now?' She was doubtful; it looked like it could rain.

'Yeah, why not? Let's take umbrellas, just in case,' he said, pointing to the umbrella stand next to the stairs near the front door. She agreed.

Veer lit a cigarette and took a drag. They had walked only a few metres when the first drop fell from the heavens above. Veer looked at Natasha, as if questioning 'should we go back?' Natasha smiled and walked ahead. Veer followed her. There was thick forest on both sides of the road. The mountain must have been dealt with some centuries back when human beings started building roads or maybe when the British came here in search of cooler weathers. On one side of the road were the mountains and on the other was a valley. The beauty of Landour was that it was still untouched by rapid commercialization, unlike Mussoorie and Shimla. Veer and Natasha were walking quietly, neither of them making any attempt to talk. Both were lost in their thoughts.

'Natasha, have you heard this: "*Tha zindagi mein marg ka khatka laga hua... Udne se peshtar bhi mera rang zard tha*"?' Veer threw away the butt of the cigarette and looked at her. It had stopped drizzling. They were a little damp as they had continued walking in the drizzle without opening the umbrellas. 'Do you know what it means?'

'Yes, I have heard this,' said Natasha, a little offended that he would think she would not know this. 'I know what it means. Ghalib says that even during our lives, we are scared of death; even before we fly, our colour becomes pale. He wants us to live more as we all have to die one day. But till then, we must live to the fullest,' she said passionately.

'Correct. Why I mentioned this is because I want to work with you and we must clear the air first,' he looked at her and she nodded in agreement.

They had reached a quaint little pizzeria by then. Veer walked in and Natasha followed. Veer seemed to be on a first-name basis with everyone. During his conversation with the manager, she realized that he had already called in the morning to reserve a table for two as he would be bringing his guest for lunch. They sat in a corner, overlooking the snow-clad mountains. Veer ordered Pasta Primavera and coffee. Natasha was not hungry, so she just ordered coffee. Veer told her in jest that he would not share his pasta with her and she should order if she wanted to eat, but she laughed it off. He ran his hand through his hair. She knew he did that when he was nervous. *Why should he be nervous?*

~

When Veer had got up in the morning, he was a little hungover. He was also uncomfortable with how he had behaved with Natasha. She was an intern and he was a senior filmmaker. She was ten years younger to him and he should not complicate his life further than it already was. He awoke feeling remorseful and decided to make amends immediately. He had been shocked when Amyra had landed up in the party—or rather, when *he* had landed up at Amyra's party—but he was privy to the producer's plan of making them work together on this film. He had been trying to get out of it, but when it didn't work out, he decided to focus on work. Amyra was a complication and he was meeting her that evening to sort that out, but Natasha was fun and he wanted to take her out for lunch. Last time they had met for dinner, he had really enjoyed himself and he wanted to let go of the negativity that seemed to be clouding their relationship and start afresh. This was his way of seeking her cooperation to start anew.

'Natasha, I want to let go of the "issues",' he said, using air quotes, 'that we have faced in the last few days. Let us focus on work for now. Of course, I hope I have not offended you with any of my words or actions, and if I have, I hope you can look past that...I hope you agree with me?' he looked at her earnestly.

After the fiasco of last night, Natasha was worried that Veer would be angry about Ishaan or would ask about her work on Guru Dutt, but he had turned a new leaf. He was in a good mood and was not looking for any explanation. She was happy that he was treating her as a friend and was focusing on her internship and learning in the process. She didn't mind. After all, she was here to learn and focus on her career.

She didn't like that Amyra had entered the dynamics, but it was not like she had any control over him. She liked him, they had kissed—but that was it. She sometimes thought that he felt more for her than he showed, but how could she know for sure? Amyra's presence complicated her life, and reminded her that he was taken, that he was a married man, and that he was a very successful filmmaker, who was married to a very beautiful and a very successful Bollywood heroine. It reminded her constantly that he was out of her league. She was briefly reminded of the movie, *She's Out of My League*. Yayu and Natasha had really liked the movie. That brought a smile to her face.

'Penny for your thoughts?' Veer asked Natasha. They had finished their lunch. Natasha had, after all, shared Veer's pasta and he had teased her about it.

'Nothing...was thinking about Yayu,' she replied.

Veer was not ready for the pang of jealousy he felt. He changed the topic immediately.

'Let's go.'

On their way back, it started raining. The beautiful trail, with tall deodar trees on both sides, became even more beautiful in the rain. Natasha had forgotten her umbrella in the restaurant. Veer opened the big purple umbrella he was carrying, and asked Natasha to come under it. Though it was a huge umbrella, it was difficult for both of them to walk under it. Natasha tried to walk closer to Veer. She tried to make light of the situation by saying, 'I am reminded of Rihanna's song "Under my umbrella...". Do you like it?'

Veer put his arms around her shoulder and said, 'Come closer or you will get wet.' Natasha could smell his cologne and feel his warm body, and how he was so tall that she barely reached his shoulders. She kept both her hands in her coat pockets and looked ahead. The rains, the music of the nature, the beating of her heart and their steps—everything was in sync. It was not a torrential rain, yet it was enough to unleash a torrent of emotions within Natasha's heart. *To hell with the internship; she wanted to kiss this gorgeous man.* She turned to him and saw his profile. He was focusing on the road ahead. She lost heart and looked in front too.

Veer, like Natasha, was having a very hard time focusing on the trail ahead. He didn't show any visible signs of discomfort, though this extreme closeness to Natasha was driving him mad with desire. She was so tiny and how perfectly she fit in with the nooks of his body. She smelled of flowers and the beach. *How could she smell of the beach in the middle of the mountains?* All he wanted to do was throw the umbrella away and kiss her. Kiss her and kiss her, till the rain kept falling on them and till their legs would support them. The bungalow was in sight and that saved him. Natasha felt that he quickened his pace a little and so did she. In fact, they practically ran the last few metres to the bungalow. Natasha and Veer vanished in different directions; they needed to be away from each other to calm down and get a grip on their emotions.

29

AFTER NEARLY ONE hour of travelling up the mountains, on the narrow, loopy road with blind turns, the whole party was about to reach Dhanaulti. The twenty-four kilometres that separated Mussoorie and Dhanaulti seemed like a lifetime to Natasha. She had motion sickness, along with vertigo. She was feeling pukish and her head was spinning. So, paling and failing against the climb of the great Himalayas, she had to pop a medicine.

When they were less than a kilometre away, Natasha asked the vehicle to be stopped. Natasha, Ishaan and Veer were travelling in the same SUV, and Riya and Amyra were following them in a second one. She was sitting in the back of the SUV and had been given the most comfortable seat by the rest of the travellers, since she was the only one who was feeling sick. Veer wanted to sit next to her and help her out…hold her hand and tell her that the journey will be over in an hour and then she would be able to enjoy the beautiful weather in Dhanaulti, but Ishaan was there to do that. Veer regretted bringing Ishaan along, who was sitting in the back with Natasha, while he sat in the front. Natasha got out of the vehicle and ran a little further away. Ishaan ran after her with a bottle of water. He held her hair as Natasha threw up.

Veer stood helplessly at a distance. He wanted to hit Ishaan, or at least do something that would help Natasha. They came back to the vehicle and began the journey again.

'It's only a few more kilometres, Natasha. Just put your head back and relax. Don't have too much water,' Veer said. Ishaan put the water bottle back in its holder. Veer made a mental note to make Ishaan suffer by making him run useless errands.

Dhanaulti was most famous for its Eco Parks—Ambar and Dhara. Big, old trees told the story of human endeavour to create the place as it presently stood. The peaks were laden with snow as far as the eye could see. Rhododendron, deodar and oak trees made up the alpine forest that cradled the park. There were some little green huts that looked like the huts of the seven dwarfs from a distance. Though it seemed close, it took another half hour to reach Eco Park.

The plan for Dhanaulti was well thought out. Veer had arranged this work trip and would have preferred to have come alone, but he had to ask Ishaan and Riya to tag along when Amyra made it clear that she would go to Dhanaulti with him 'for old times' sake'. They used to come to Dhanaulti often when they were newly married and needed to run away from the hustle-bustle of the maddening crowd of Mumbai. With the rider in the contract and their meeting that day, Veer had decided that they would have a congenial working relationship. So, to make sure that he didn't have to deal with Amyra too much, he asked the rest to tag along.

Veer had asked everyone to come along, but he was reluctant to ask Natasha. He didn't trust himself with her around. Her innocence and her beauty, both drove him crazy…made him lose perspective. Yet, he wanted to bring her along. She was like a younger version of him. She reminded him of all that is good in life, of hope and how far he had come.

The cottages of the Eco Park were situated amidst greenery and undulating hillocks. Veer had booked three cottages in Ambar. One for Natasha and Ishaan, the second for Amyra and Riya, and the last one he would have to himself. The first two cottages were situated close to each other and the last one was a hundred metres away. He had done that on purpose. He intended to work, and he needed to be alone for that.

As soon as they reached Ambar, Natasha was immediately shown to her bedroom. Each cottage had two separate bedrooms with attached baths, a drawing room, and a small pantry. The bedrooms were very beautifully done and gave the feel of the British era, with canopied beds, archaic furniture and big paintings. Ishaan was excited that he was sharing the cottage with Natasha and that irritated Veer. Amyra was not too happy about staying with Riya, but she didn't express it. The rest were also shown their respective rooms and were informed that lunch would be served in Veer's cottage shortly, which he had ordered, and he asked them to join him once they were fresh and ready.

Natasha was lying on her stomach on the bed. Her eyes were closed and the light from the fireplace was not only imparting a beautiful glow to the room, but also adding warmth. She felt like she was dying, not only because she had thrown up but also because of making a scene while the rest of the women of Bollywood seemed lady-like and composed. *Why did she have to throw up? What would Veer think?* The last few weeks had transformed her life. From being a movie enthusiast and a student of movie-making, to gallivanting with Bollywood bigwigs, her life was the stuff that dreams are made of.

Natasha didn't like Amyra. She was beautiful—perfect. She could see why Veer would be in love with her. She was sexy and feminine; almost feral in her grace and gait. Her five-feet, ten-inch frame was reed-thin but adequately endowed when it came to the assets. Her thin frame made her look dainty and ladylike at the same time. She didn't like when Amyra spoke to Veer; her husky voice melted like honey on one's ear; her laughter was music to the ears. One look at her and she knew why Veer had fallen in love with her or why *anyone* would fall in love with her. She was the dream girl to the boys of her generation. She didn't like that Amyra knew Veer better than her. She didn't like that Veer loved her. She didn't like that *she* happened first. She didn't like Amyra.

She didn't have to like Amyra. She just had to learn to get by. She had to make that effort! She must get up, put on fresh clothes, a little makeup and be grateful to God for this opportunity. She had never, even in the best of her dreams, ever imagined that so much will happen so quickly in her life. She had never thought that she would get the break of a lifetime so early in her career.

Natasha got up and took a shower. She chose a fresh pair of jeans and a red Zara sweater that her friends said was quite a steal. She had been complimented many a times for looking gorgeous in that sweater. She put on the crimson L'oreal non-transfer lip colour, which she had spent a bomb on. A pair of black boots—a first copy of Aldo boots, which she had picked up from Lajpat Nagar—completed her look. A spray of Clinique Happy pepped her up and she was ready to go. She looked at her reflection in the mirror and liked what she saw. She locked her room and walked out of the cottage, feeling confident about her look.

The walk up to Veer's cottage worked up her appetite. She had not eaten anything since the morning for fear of throwing up.

Veer's cottage was bigger and looked more like a British bungalow than a cottage. Her steps quickened a bit when she heard laughter and music echo from the cottage.

It looked like a proper party, with music and dancing. Robbie Williams was singing 'Have You Met Miss Jones' on the music system, and Riya and Ishaan were twirling around the room as Amyra looked on, with a glass of wine in her hand. Amyra was sitting next to the fireplace in a big comfortable chair, looking radiant. She was wearing a pair of blue jeans, a beige sweater and a red scarf, and her beautiful hair sculpted her perfect face. *Why did I even make the effort*? Natasha thought. Even when she was casually dressed, Amyra looked like she was on the spread of an international magazine. Amyra signalled her to the dining table. It was laden with various kinds of bread, cheese, fruit, pasta, curry, salad and pastry. She was informed that the rest had had their lunch and she should also go ahead. Veer was nowhere to be seen but she didn't think it was appropriate to ask about Veer's whereabouts, so she put some food on her plate. There was so much to choose from that Natasha got confused and just took some pasta and bread. She filled a glass with red wine and sat away from Amyra, towards the door.

The sumptuous lunch and good music had lifted her spirits and she was looking forward to working in the evening. Veer had asked her to proofread some of the scenes and point out errors, if any. She had already laid them out before coming for lunch. She just wanted Veer to spell out what the plans for the rest of the days were. There was a lot of ambiguity about their trip to Dhanaulti. She had tried speaking to Veer about it, but when she realized that the whole lot of them were going, and that they were going to work, she decided to tag along.

'Hey, you guys are still here?' Veer walked in. 'I hope you all had lunch,' he said, looking at Natasha. Natasha nodded as the rest confirmed.

'Where were you?' asked Riya.

Natasha saw how Amyra's body language changed as Veer entered the room. *What was going on? Weren't they over?*

'I had gone to pick up some cigarettes and it turned out that none of the shops around the park sell them, so I had to walk a few kilometres before I could locate these.' He showed the packets he was carrying.

'You should quit, Veer,' Amyra said, 'It's not good for your health.' Amyra looked directly at him. The room fell quiet for a moment and then Veer replied. 'I will. I haven't found a reason to quit yet.'

'So, what's the plan now?' Riya asked, sounding exasperated. 'Are we going to sit here for the rest of the day?'

'No. I will work, and you guys can go sightseeing. Dhanaulti is a beautiful place and you must enjoy the beauty of it. We will meet in the evening for dinner and then we will discuss work,' Veer replied with such clarity that everybody knew that they had to leave then. Amyra stayed put in her seat. As the rest of them were leaving, Veer called Natasha over. He handed her a packet of goodies comprising M&M's, Gems, assorted candies, gummy bears and the good old Hajmola.

'I hope you are feeling better now. I found these at the shop and thought they might help you if you feel pukish again. Also, I picked up a strip of Avomine tablets. You must have one half an hour before you start any car journey,' Veer said, looking at her with affection. Natasha took the packet sheepishly and left.

30

EVERYBODY LEFT BUT Amyra stayed back. Veer had gone to his bedroom to change. He had asked the room service to clear the food and asked the housekeeping to clean up. Amyra had wanted to talk to him, but he had been very elusive since their last meeting. She had met him in Marriott that evening, and he had only agreed after she insisted very strongly. She had taken a lot of pains to plan out her visit to Landour and to meet Veer. She had also tried to reach him through her lawyer and her friends, but when all efforts failed, she hauled ass and came to Landour so Veer would be forced to take notice.

She had planned the party meticulously. Riya had been sceptical when she had first heard Amyra's idea but had come through when the latter had informed her that she had made sure that the producer would convince Veer to take her as the second lead. Riya, who, despite being a top model, was failing to find a decent director to debut with, had been easily persuaded. The rest of the gang was anyway going to be there for the shooting of the film, so they had played along. In fact, many of them had genuinely wanted to meet Veer. And last but not the least, the lure of free booze never fails to motivate the young crowd and Amyra knew that.

She had been surprised when he had entered with a girl. That she was a 'plain, little chick' as Riya had described Natasha later, gave her confidence. She had been very sure that she would be able to speak to Veer at the party, but that didn't work. He was not listening to her, telling her, clearly, to stay away and warning her that he didn't want to create a scene. He had also told her that it would be best if the both of them kept up the pretences for the sake of the movie. She had followed through and stayed aloof on the promise that he would meet her the following evening at Marriott. What had enraged her was the way Veer looked at Natasha. She knew that look. It nearly broke Amyra.

She was not here to mend fences. She was not here because of his new movie. His winning the National Award mattered to her only because it brought him name and fame. His success had always been important to her—not because that made him worth her, but because she knew his potential and was happy when he had realized it. She was here because she still loved him and wanted him back, but she couldn't tell him that. Not just yet.

Veer was taking a bath. She could hear the shower running. She lay down on the bed in his room. The end of a marriage is a very painful thing. It's as painful as the death of a loved one. Amyra had loved Veer with all her heart. She was sure that he had reciprocated with the same fervour. But it was not enough. Love was not enough. They were too young and naïve to believe that love is enough for a marriage to be successful. She had never thought that Veer could be insecure. Insecure about his work... insecure about her work... her working with male stars. They were in the business of pretending; somewhere down the line, they had started pretending to each other. There were fundamental problems with their marriage that both of them refused to look at. He had started internalizing everything and brooding. She had started looking for excuses to stay away. They continued to be polite with each other but then one day, all hell broke loose.

'What are you doing here?'

Veer came out from the bathroom. A big, fluffy white towel was wrapped around his waist, hiding his modesty. Water was glistening on his torso and on his hair. Amyra had forgotten about his raw sexuality...his sheer manliness...his perfect body. Her stomach lurched.

'I wanted to speak to you.' Amyra looked away from his chest.

Veer started wearing the clothes he had already laid out on the bed. He had worn jeans and wrapped the towel around his shoulders. Amyra was tempted to touch him.

'Veer, come here,' she signalled to the pillow next to hers.

He didn't reply and put on his T-shirt and sweater. He rubbed his hair with the towel one last time, before he carelessly threw it on the armchair next to the fireplace. He went and lay next to Amyra.

'What is it, Amyra?' he asked.

'Veer, I have been trying to speak to you. You are not giving me a chance. We need to talk, Veer,' she pleaded. 'Veer...' she couldn't say anything more. Tears rolled down her eyes. Veer reached forward to wipe them.

'Let's not talk, Amyra. Let's just be,' he said, running a hand through his hair. Amyra was sitting up now. She was determined to talk. *It would have to be right now.*

'No, Veer. Please hear me out.' She wiped her tears with the back of her hand like a little girl.

Something inside Veer reacted to that. She was that same girl—the girl who he had loved like a crazy fool...the girl who meant everything in the world to him...the girl who had helped him achieve his potential. She was also the girl who broke his heart, who didn't refute the charges of wife battery that were thrown at him by the media and the police. She saw him go through all that and didn't say a word. *He didn't have to hear her out.* But then she came forward and hugged him. And he realized that she was silently crying.

'Okay, tell me. What is it that you want to say to me?' He had had enough of her crying.

'Veer, please forgive me. Let's give our marriage another chance... Please... I still love you. I know you love me too. We must give our relationship a chance,' she begged.

She had come all this way because she wanted Veer back in her life and she was willing to go to any lengths for it. She was still sitting very close to him. Amyra leaned forward and lightly kissed his lips. When Veer didn't rebuff her, she became bolder and claimed his lips completely. A familiar excitement rushed through Veer and he kissed her back. He wanted more. It had been ages. His hands were all over her. She moaned as he bit her lower lip. That excited him further and he reached inside her sweater to cup her breasts. They were kissing each other and taking off their clothes at the same time. Then Amyra looked at him. He was hesitating.

She urged him on, 'Please, Veer.'

The warmth of the room and the comfort of the known were driving them crazy with desire. Veer could only think about the beautiful woman, who was still his wife, pleading with him to take her. He was on top of her, looking into her eyes, seeking her permission, when suddenly there was a loud banging on the door.

31

NATASHA HAD LEFT Veer's cottage in a rush. She didn't want anyone to see the glee on her face. He had not only been supportive of her, but also remembered to bring some goodies for her. That sweet gesture had won her over. She had been a little heartbroken when she had walked into his cottage only to realize that he wasn't around. Amyra's looking regal hadn't helped either. Also, he hadn't looked at her when he had walked in, but he had noticed the rest and nodded at Amyra. She had wondered if she even belonged in that Bollywood gathering. Then Veer had called her over and showed her that he cared.

She knew that lately her mood had been contingent upon Veer's behaviour towards her. She also knew that these emotional ups and downs showed a lot of emotional investment on her part in her relationship with Veer. This was not good for her working relationship. She was trying to be aloof and focusing on her learnings, but that was easier said than done. She felt that she saw something in Veer's eyes... something for her. But she couldn't be sure.

She had to go to her cottage but she decided to go for a walk instead. Tall deodar trees lined up on both sides of the mountain road. She had put her earphones on to play the music of her choice, and was thinking about Veer. She had realized that she loved him, sometime back in Landour. She had fallen in love with him way before they had kissed, but it was clear to her that her feelings ran deeper when she saw him with Amyra. Her presence had made Natasha realize that Veer was the quintessential 'forbidden fruit'. He was rich, successful, senior—in age and in career—and married. Even if her affection was returned by him, she would always be tagged as a 'gold digger', an 'opportunist' and someone who used sex to get ahead in her career. Incidentally, she did not care too much about such tags. She never had.

She had not spoken to anyone about her feelings—not Nani, not even Yayu. She wanted to come clean to someone about what was happening, but what would she say? There would be so much judgment heaped upon her if she told anyone about it. She often wondered if Nani would understand. She knew Yayu would, but would he help her convince Nani? She could make the whole world understand, but what about Veer? He was still married, and if that was not enough, the lady in question was very much in the picture and on the spot, and he didn't seem to mind. She had seen how her body language changed when he was around, but she had also seen something different about him when she was around. Both of them made a beautiful pair and would reign over the industry if they came back together. *Did Amyra and Veer want that?* Natasha was still mulling over why he did not say 'no' to the producer and take a heroine of his choice. He could have stood his ground if he really wanted to, but *did* he want to? She was sure, somewhere deep in her heart, that Veer wanted to work with Amyra again.

Natasha had been walking for nearly an hour. The songs stopped playing. When she looked at the phone, she realized that only 15 per cent battery was left and the phone was asking her to preserve the rest. She was far away from the Eco Park and it was already 5:30 in the evening. Darkness descends on hills faster than it does in plains. It was dusky already, and was becoming darker every moment. Natasha decided to turn back and walk on the same trail that she had been walking on for the last one hour. She looked at her phone again. The battery was nearly discharged. She started walking faster.

The phantom-white mountains stood against the sky, with reared heads. The white snow shone where the moonlight caressed them. It was a clear sky with millions of stars twinkling in full glory. Not a single cloud could be seen in the expanse. She could see twinkling yellowish lights on the hillside, which were either road lights or lights from the houses. The hill people were simple, hardworking people who had to struggle each day for survival. With the cloudburst in Uttarkashi last month, tourism in the whole state of Uttarakhand had been affected and that explained why there were so few people on the streets. In fact, on her way back, Natasha could not find a single tourist. She did find a rickety little paan shop, which also sold bread-omelette and ginger tea. The smell of the food got to her and she decided to have a cup of tea before proceeding.

∽

Ishaan had searched for Natasha everywhere and tried to call her, but to no avail. He got worried and ran over to Veer's cottage. He knocked a few times but there was no response, so this time, he banged loudly.

'What?' Veer had opened the door. Amyra was standing behind him. They had thrown on their clothes very quickly. Veer was visibly shaken.

How could he have let his basic instincts take charge of him? His relationship with Amyra was anything but simple. He couldn't complicate it further. As far as he was concerned, their marriage was over. He couldn't lead her on. Wonder what had gotten into her to have pulled such a stunt!

Ishaan wondered what was going on between the two of them, but he had bigger issues on his mind.

'Sir, Natasha is nowhere to be found. Her phone is also switched off. I have searched everywhere and I didn't know what to do,' Ishaan replied helplessly.

'Since when has she been missing?' Veer asked, already putting on his shoes.

Ishaan informed him that she had gone for a walk immediately after lunch. Veer looked at the time.

'But it's half past 8 now. Why didn't you tell me earlier?' he questioned Ishaan, now putting on his jacket.

'Sir, I was looking for her. I didn't want to disturb you. When I couldn't locate her on the property and around, I panicked and came to you,' Ishaan replied.

Amyra was still standing in the middle of the room, when Veer walked out with Ishaan.

~

Natasha had been walking like a headless chicken for a long time now. Somehow, she had lost her way after leaving the paan shop. She had walked out of the shop, fairly confident of the route to her cottage, but somewhere along the way, she had taken a wrong turn and that had been her undoing. Her phone had also died; she just didn't know what to do. She was now in the middle of the forest and could feel that she was not very far from the Eco Park or her cottage, but she really didn't know which way to go. She saw a small bench near a big deodar tree and sat down on it to rest a little. Moonlight lit up the puddles of water around the bench on the pathway. She could see the reflection of the sky in one of the puddles. While she was enjoying the view, she was also worried about getting back to her cottage. She heard a loud rumbling and looked around with a start. A branch fell away from the tree and landed with a thud on the ground. She thought she could see some people approaching, and became a little stiff with nervousness. She could make out two figures. Definitely men, as both looked tall. One of them was stocky and the other one was lean. Each of them had a torch in their hand. Natasha instinctively looked for and found a thick stick to use as a weapon if either of the figures would try to attack her.

The figures came closer and threw the torchlight on her face.

She screamed, 'Hey, who's that? Don't do that!'

'Natasha, it's us!' Ishaan ran forward and hugged her. 'Where the hell have you been? We have been looking for you for so long? Do you even know what time it is?'

Veer had come over to her and was fuming with anger, 'What the hell do you think you are doing, Natasha? You have had all of us worried for nearly five hours now. It's bloody late.'

Natasha had never seen him so angry. She was very tired from all the walking and emotionally drained from the fear of being lost. When Veer screamed at her, she started crying. Ishaan was standing close to her and tried to console her, but what happened next, shocked Ishaan. Veer came up to Natasha and hugged her. He hugged her tightly and kissed her on her forehead. Natasha had stopped crying, but he was feeling very bad for having screamed at her. He was so relieved when he had seen her sitting on that bench. He had not realized what this chit of a girl had begun to mean to him, till there was a threat of losing her.

'Don't cry. We are here now. We have found you and we will take you back to civilization,' Veer said.

He was about to give her the kiss of her life when he realized that they had company. He tried to make light of the situation by suggesting that they start walking back as the dinner must be getting cold. He let go of her and they started walking back. She realized that she hadn't really been very far from the cottages.

'I would have come back eventually. I wasn't very far,' she said, being obstinate. Both Veer and Ishaan laughed out loud.

'There you are! We were sick with worry!' The happy trio was bombarded with angry questions as they entered Veer's cottage. Amyra walked up to Veer and hugged him. He told her that they had found Natasha sitting very close to the cottage, so she would have eventually come back. Ishaan laughed out loud, but Natasha was irritated. She did not want to be laughed at in front of Amyra and Riya.

'Can I be excused? I want to go to my room,' Natasha said angrily. She was tired and hungry and not at all in the mood to deal with Amyra and Riya.

'No, you may not,' replied Veer, 'you owe us a dinner in your company for labouring so hard to find you.'

Veer was grinning. He was in a good mood now. Natasha was safe and she was with him. He had had the fright of his life when she was lost. All kinds of thoughts had crossed his mind and that had made him certain that Natasha meant more to him than he had thought she did. *Was he in love with her? Really in love?*

32

'DEKHI ZAMAANE KI *yaari, bichhade sabhi bari bari...'*

Guru Dutt sang the melodious number on the projector screen propped up in Veer's bedroom. Amyra, Riya, Ishaan and Natasha were lying on the bed, wrapped up in thick blankets, but Veer was sitting in an armchair next to the fireplace. It was midnight by the time the dinner got over, and the group had wanted to relax a bit. They talked about how, in college, they used to have 'night outs' watching movies, and then there would be a bet to see who could last through the night. Veer had recommended watching the movie *Kaagaz Ke Phool* as 'there was a lot to be learnt from it'. All of them had watched it many times and had fallen asleep one by one. Natasha was awake and so was Veer. As the last scene of the movie rolled out with Guru Dutt dying in the director's chair in a deserted studio, a broken and forgotten man, Natasha wiped a tear and got up from the bed.

Veer turned off the projector and darkness suddenly descended upon the room. Natasha was looking for her shoes and was not able to locate them. She tumbled and Veer caught her. He led her out of the room, and she followed him obediently. He took her to the other bedroom in the cottage. She followed. Her heart was beating so loudly, she was sure he could hear it. His room was both grand and cozy. It was appropriately heated and the yellowish light emitting from the lamp made it look inviting. Veer took her to the fireplace and turned around to look at her.

'I have been meaning to do this since the evening...' *He was going to kiss her. He needed to kiss her to clear his mind and to decide how he really felt about her. That kiss with Amyra had really messed him up.*

She could see it in his eyes. They were full of desire, but she could also see a hint of affection. She didn't want to think at all. She wanted to grab the moment and she did. She needed to know what it would be like to kiss him again. She had dwelled on it, night after night. She would finally know.

He tilted his head a little and lightly brushed her lips. Natasha tilted her head to give him more access. His hand was on her back and with the other, he pulled off her shawl. He kissed her. Her body heated up instantly. His lips were becoming more insistent and Natasha was also becoming more aggressive in her response. Her hands were running up and down his back, holding on to him. His tongue lightly brushed her lower lip and she let his tongue claim hers. His hand was holding her closer to him, even more tightly. This was not a simple kiss. It demanded more. It knocked her wind out. She broke the kiss and hugged him. He nuzzled her neck and sent shivers down her spine. He was not letting go. She just had to give a signal that she didn't want this and he would stop, but her body was moulding itself to his body.

This was different. She was different. She was Natasha. He wanted to please her. She was so new at this. He wanted to teach her. He wanted to keep doing this to her and never stop. At that moment, he knew he loved her. He didn't feel any remorse in kissing Natasha. It felt natural. It was right. She was the perfect fit for him.

Natasha knew she must put a stop to this, but a more physical and animalistic need was taking over her. She was unable to carry on. She might not have been in her senses entirely, but Natasha was still able to think. She knew that if they continued like this, there would be no looking back. She looked up at him. His eyes were dark. She could see desire in them, but she knew what she had to do.

'Veer, let's not complicate things,' she said with a heavy heart. She didn't want anything more than for Veer to love her, but not like this. 'We have to work together and this will unnecessarily complicate our relationship, don't you think?'

Natasha had distanced herself from him. Her body was pulsing; her legs were unsteady. She had to remind herself that this would not be an easy relationship. He was still married, his wife was here and, above all, he was her boss. No matter how badly drawn she was to him, she had to rein her emotions in.

Veer's body was throbbing with unmet desire, but there was clarity in his eyes now. The confusion had vanished. She was stunning. Her beauty, her poise, her innocence and, above all, her character, drew him to her like a moth to a flame. He had held himself back for a long time, but she had overwhelmed him this evening. Just a day before, he had made peace with the fact that they should have a healthy working relationship and not complicate things, yet he lost control. *What had gotten into him? He must get a grip on himself.*

'Of course, you are right. Come, I will walk you to your cottage,' he said, turning towards the door.

She could see that he was angry; she couldn't blame him. She, too, was feeling angry and frustrated.

'That should prove to us, though, that we better keep our distance till we are working on this project,' Natasha said, wrapping her shawl around as a muffler and closing the coat buttons in front. Her hands were still shaking and her lips were feeling swollen. She knew that her nipples were erect, but she could feel emptiness in the pit of her stomach. She still wanted him.

Veer was walking next to her with his hands in his pockets.

'Natasha, I didn't force you into anything,' he said, feeling irritated.

'No, Veer, you didn't. I am totally responsible for my actions.'

Veer couldn't argue with honesty. Also, he didn't have the strength to argue with her. He was still reeling under the havoc that their kiss had caused to his system, though the anger was helping him negate that. They walked in silence. Both of them knew that they had gotten over just a hump and there would be steeper mountains to scale. They had reached her cottage. Veer nodded at Natasha and left.

~

Amyra woke up. When she did not find Veer around, she went looking for him. She called his name, but there was no response. She had noticed that Natasha was also missing from the room. An unknown fear gripped her heart. She didn't know what she expected but the fear of what could happen was paralyzing her. She had seen how Veer looked at Natasha and how worried he had become when he had heard of her being lost. She knew there was something going on. She also knew that Natasha liked him. Any young girl with a heart and an ambition in cinema would love him.

She had left Veer, but he had not left her heart. She had tried to let go of him, but their past had its claws buried deep inside her. She had worked so hard that she would not get even a moment to think about her failed relationship. Amyra was heartbroken when Veer had been branded a wife-beater and ridiculed in the press. They definitely had had bad times and he had raised his hand, but she knew that was out of passion. She knew that he had reacted violently because he loved her like that. He had tried to reason it out with her, but she just didn't let him. She was so fixated upon the idea of being free, that she didn't realize that what she was seeking was not freedom, but a descend into doom. The moment people in the industry got a whiff of her troubled relationship, there were umpteen sympathizers. She had tried to find solace in the arms of other men—some offering their shoulder to cry on; some offering their villas to party in and forget her grief—but nearly all wanted to get intimate with her; something she didn't want. Her only mistake was that she never refuted any charges when Veer was put on a media trial, but she was going to correct that by taking all her cases back and quashing the FIRs. *She wanted Veer back. She really did.*

The door to the other room was open. She couldn't hear anything. The cottage was absolutely silent. Amyra looked inside from the side of the door. Natasha and Veer were locked in a passionate embrace, kissing. She looked on as he kissed her more passionately. Something welled up and broke inside her. She didn't say anything, but just left the cottage and walked back to hers.

33

THE NEXT FEW days were only about work. Veer was locked up in his room, working on the script and the rest were doing whatever research he had asked them to do. Amyra had planned the shooting of a commercial for a shampoo brand in Dhanaulti. The producers of the ad film were not very excited about shooting in the mountains, but didn't have a choice when the brand ambassador threatened to pull out. Amyra was, after all, the reigning queen of Bollywood. She had also brought along the script that she was going to work on next. It was a Raghu Ravindran film and Amyra was really excited about it, as he had had a very good track record. Her PR team and her assistants were reminding her every day that she had to be back in Mumbai in the beginning of the coming week. Amyra was focused; that little escapade that she had seen between Veer and Natasha had made her pull herself back, but only for a bit. During the next few days, she observed very carefully that Veer and Natasha kept their distance from each other. She had thought that she would leave everything and go back to Mumbai, but the wife in her didn't want to give up. She had gone over each and every moment spent with Veer since she had come to know him, and had decided their relationship was worth fighting for. She had decided to give Veer time to get used to her being around. Steadily but surely, she was planning to make inroads into his heart again.

Amyra planned an outing for all of them at Adventure Zone. She couldn't have gone there when there were tourists, so she pulled a few strings to get the whole place to themselves. Who can say 'no' to the top heroine of the silver screen? Veer was reluctant to get away from his room, but Amyra knew how to make him agree to her plan. She had done that many times and knew what worked on Veer. All his excuses of working on the script were met with, 'I know, but this is a team activity and builds confidence. I insist that we do this as a team. Won't you do it for me?' and Veer gave in. Amyra could be really persuasive if she wanted to. She was also banking on her power to persuade to lead Veer back into her arms.

Once the plan was laid out, she wanted Natasha to be left behind. So, when it came to asking her, Amyra said, 'Natasha, we'll be skywalking. Would you like to join us? Though, I must inform you that the instructor I spoke to on the phone made it clear that anyone with medical issues, including vertigo, will not be permitted to do it. So, I think travelling to the Adventure Zone is a waste of time for you, but the decision is yours to make. I wouldn't want to stop you, if you want to come.'

Natasha realized that Amyra didn't want her to be around. She had noticed in the last few days that Amyra and Veer were on friendlier terms than they had been when the trip had begun. In fact, she had seen that Amyra spent most of her time, when she was not working, in his cottage. It was not a surprise that they were spending time together, but it was surprising that Amyra would make so much effort to bring Veer around. All that she had read about the both of them in newspapers and magazines had led her to believe that they were very bitter with each other and had parted on really bad terms, but what she saw was the exact opposite. When she was with them in the same room, she could see the affection one had for the other. It was quite obvious that there were still feelings involved, but she could not quite understand what Veer's stand was. She could see what Amyra was working towards, but she could not read Veer's mind. In the beginning, she had thought that it was only because the producers had insisted that he had brought Amyra along. Veer had shown concern for Natasha and had shown romantic interest in her and that had led Natasha to believe that he might not have any feelings for Amyra, but that was not the case. He clearly still did. She had dealt with loss enough in her lifetime to understand that marriage was a serious business and required commitment and hard work. With any relationship—more so with marriage—many distractions and indiscretions happen, but they are ultimately forgiven and forgotten in favour of protecting the institution of marriage. Maybe Amyra and Veer needed a second chance at their relationship. Maybe it would turn out that they still loved each other. With a heavy heart, Natasha decided that she was but an intern, and she should know her place.

Since that night, Veer had kept his distance from her. She did feel that Veer's aloofness was something she had brought on herself, but she had no regrets. She was focused on her career, and emotions were a complication that she wasn't willing to bring into her working relationship. He had not been alone with her, even for a single second. If he wanted any research or proofreading to be done, he would message the instructions or drop an email. Even when they were in a group, he restricted himself to talking to Riya, Ishaan and Amyra. Natasha didn't mind. She had insisted that they keep it uncomplicated and he was following through. Yet, when he was in the room, she wished he would look at her and single her out. That he would speak only to her. That he would kiss her again, and again. And again. So, even when she wanted to say 'yes', she decided to sit it out.

~

Early next morning when their gear and picnic baskets were being loaded, Veer couldn't see Natasha. It was still dark, as the sun was not up yet. Amyra informed him that she wasn't coming along because of vertigo. He asked Ishaan about her whereabouts, to which he gave a vague reply. Veer decided to check it out himself. He walked up to Natasha's cottage. His heart was hammering inside. He had not spoken to her properly since that day. It had been difficult but he had to respect her wishes. Whenever he saw her around, it was physical pain that he went through, trying to stop himself from reaching out and touching her. The way her eyes lit up when he was discussing camera techniques or narrating a story from his previous experiences melted his heart. She was so young and eager to learn; he could not burden her with the yearnings of his heart and the baggage of his failed marriage with Amyra. He had to keep his distance, lest he touch her or do something stupid. He could not understand how he could lose control in front of this magical girl even at his age. He thought infatuations were a thing of the past, but Natasha had made him aware of his limitations as a human being—as a man.

He knocked on the door. Once. Twice. The third time, he called her name out as well. Natasha was asleep, but the way her name came out from his mouth stirred something deep inside her. Natasha opened the door; her dark hair was dishevelled and surrounded her pretty face like a halo. She was wearing comfortable flannel pyjamas and a hoodie. The room was very warm as the fire had been burning in the fireplace through the night. Veer nearly lost control; her body was radiating heat.

'Natasha, why aren't you ready? Aren't you coming with us to Adventure Zone?' Veer asked, trying to not look at her directly.

'Good morning,' she smiled, 'I am not coming for the trip. You know I have vertigo and travelling on the mountainous roads is too much for me. So, I will sit this one out.'

Natasha collected all her hair and started twisting it in to a bun on top of her head. That simple act of tying her hair made her look absolutely sexy. Veer had to look away. He just wanted to reach out and kiss her till she would agree to let him do more. Instead, he pulled out his authority card and said, 'You are coming along and that's final. You have ten minutes to get ready. We are waiting outside. Hurry up,' and he left.

The next ten minutes were like a one-minute-military-drill-times-ten. Natasha quickly went through the business of taking a bath and getting ready. She was one of those whose day began only after she had taken a bath. Yayu always teased her about it. He didn't really believe in bathing, especially in winters. Natasha rummaged through her clothes and decided on a pair of black chinos, layered a T-shirt underneath a sweater, and a feather-light yellow jacket from Woodland completed her adventure look. With her big bag on one shoulder and her practical-yet-trendy fuchsia sneakers adorning her feet, Natasha was ready to take on the world. There was a distinct spring in her step because Veer had asked her to come along. All her resolution to stay away had gone kaput the moment he said 'you are coming along'. If Amyra didn't want her around, it was her problem, not Natasha's.

Through the journey to the Adventure Zone, Natasha felt giddy but her resolve and her willpower helped her steer the course without puking. She was really praying to God to help her get through the six kilometres that separated the Eco Park and Adventure Zone without making a fool of herself. Once there, the stunning view of the mountains and the Doon Valley overwhelmed all of them with its beauty. Deodar, blue pine and oak trees sprouted wherever they could, giving the slopes a 'Swiss Alps' feel. Natasha also spotted a few apple trees. The guide pointed out the peaks of Top Tibba and Tapowan, and also informed them that during winters, the famous 'winter line' could also be seen from there.

The adventure park provided a hoard of activities, like skywalking, sky bridge, flying fox, zip line, trekking, paint ball, mountain biking, quad biking, rock climbing and paragliding. Once they were through with filling the medical forms and other undertakings, the owner of the place came over. He was smitten with Amyra and couldn't get over the fact that she had descended upon his property. He handled everything related to Amyra personally. Natasha was amused to see how grown-up men make a fool of themselves in front a woman who they barely know but were besotted with. She saw how Veer remained aloof and didn't speak much. The management had planned the whole day for them with multiple activities in the morning, followed by lunch, and then some more activities in the afternoon.

While the rest tried out skywalking, flying fox and other activities that involved walking at or swinging from a height, Natasha took their pictures. She just couldn't bring herself to do any of that, but when it came to paintball or quad biking she was the first one to put on the gear. Despite her reservations, she was having fun. Veer was quite an adventure freak and it turned out that Amyra and Veer used to be adventure junkies and had travelled the world in search of such thrill. They had even bungee jumped at one of the highest bungee jumping sites in the world, the Nevis Bungy in New Zealand. On any trip that they had taken—be it for work or pleasure—they had always planned an adventure element. Looking at how they were bonding over the skywalking, Natasha felt inadequate. *How could a man, who looked for thrill in free-falling and who sought adventure any which way he could, be interested in a girl who had vertigo? It was definitely not meant to be.*

After lunch, paragliding had been planned. They were to go as couples. First, Amyra and Veer went, then Riya and Ishaan went, and then, when it came to Natasha, she refused because of her fear of heights. Amyra and Riya were being impatient and wanted to move on to the next activity, but Veer really wanted Natasha to try it. When she was still not convinced, Veer told the instructor that he would fly with her. As they got ready, Veer told Natasha to stay calm and trust him. He told her that he would not let any harm come to her, ever. The way he said it made her believe him. As they took the leap of faith, Natasha closed her eyes. She was in front and Veer was handling the glider. He could feel how tense her body was. But once they were airborne, Natasha realized the most difficult part was the jump; after that, the flight was relaxing and enlightening. Veer asked her to open her eyes and relax. They were flying over the hills and valleys of Dhanaulti. Once she relaxed, Natasha started enjoying the flight. She was giggling with pleasure, like a little girl. Veer's heart was exploding with all the emotions he felt for her. He wanted to make her this happy always. When it was time to land, Veer started making a figure of eight in the air to lose altitude and when he was lined up, he applied the brakes. He told Natasha to move her legs as if she were running, because when they would hit the earth, they would still be under momentum from the flight. Natasha did what he asked and screamed with excitement as they hit the land. Once the movement stopped, she turned around to face him and hugged him. He returned the hug and kissed her on the forehead.

'Yay! I did it,' she shouted it out loud to anyone who was listening. Ishaan came forward to hug her.

'See, I told you, it's not that difficult,' Ishaan said, helping her to come out from the harness.

With one flight under her belt, Natasha was willing to let her heart soar, but while they were flying, Amyra had decided to cut their flight short and end the story there and then. Both were unaware of the decision each had taken, but both were determined. On their journey back, Amyra and Veer sat in one SUV and the rest in another, and when they reached the cottages, Natasha realized that the other vehicle had taken a detour somewhere on the way. *What was Amyra up to?*

34

AFTER A RELAXED bath and a big mug of coffee, Natasha again thought of checking on Veer and Amyra. She knew that their vehicle had taken a detour before entering Dhanaulti, but she didn't check with Riya or Ishaan. She was sure that the both of them would know if Veer and Amyra had any plans, but she couldn't bring herself to ask. She decided to relax and hoped that they would be back by dinner time. She had had a wonderful time in the adventure park. All her fears of falling sick and not feeling too well had been allayed. Veer had been very supportive. She loved how he had taken her on her maiden paragliding flight. She had been petrified of taking the jump, but Veer had guided her through and held her arms from his seat behind her. He had told her to believe him…to believe that all will be well…that she would love flying like a bird. When she had finally taken the plunge, Veer had continuously reminded her that he would be with her, till she had calmed down and realized that they were flying. The beautiful scenery had taken her breath away. She had seen mountain goats lazily grazing in the lush green valley, children running up the hills and miniature cars riding up and down the loopy roads. She had also seen the sun on the horizon.

The sky had a beautiful orange, yellow and pinkish hue to it as the sun readied to set.

Natasha had loved everything about flying with Veer. Her heart had been singing, soaring, as she flew with Veer. She hadn't wanted the flight to end. She had been in a dream where Veer was hers, but she knew, once she had landed, that the reality would take over. They had flown for about forty-five minutes when Veer had said that the sun was setting and it would be best if they landed. All good things come to an end and so had her flight, but she was happy that it had happened. Would she feel the same when this internship would come to an end? She had lost her heart to a man way out of her league. Her heart would definitely be broken. Or would it be?

With so many thoughts clouding her mind, Natasha walked up to Veer's cottage in search of both him and dinner. She had not eaten much in the park for fear of throwing up and now her stomach was rumbling with hunger. Natasha could hear Carrie Underwood singing 'Home Sweet Home' on the music system in the drawing room. She opened the door to find Riya sitting on Ishaan's lap and kissing him. When they realized Natasha had entered, Riya looked up and said, 'Hello'. Ishaan looked a little embarrassed, but Riya was nonchalant about it. Natasha was shocked to find them like that, but didn't show it. She had seen some chemistry developing between Ishaan and Riya, but hadn't realized it had progressed that much. *No wonder Ishaan was never around! He was always in Riya's cottage.*

Natasha asked about Veer and Amyra, and Riya informed her that they were not there yet.

'Natasha, I think Amyra has taken Veer to their favourite hotel in Dhanaulti. She booked a honeymoon suite last night. I am sure you can understand what her plans are. She really wants Veer to come back to her. Don't you think they belong together?'

Riya got up from Ishaan's lap and walked up to the dining table. It was laid out for a formal dinner but Riya only filled wine in a glass and came back to the sofa next to Ishaan. Natasha was still standing glued to the ground. She was not prepared for what Riya had said. It was like being hit by a bullet. She had known Amyra's plans since she had come to Landour, but so much had happened between Veer and her since then. She was so caught up in the business of her heart that she never thought that Amyra and Veer could get back together. *Could they get back together?* Natasha was not hungry anymore, but she put some food on her plate and tried to eat anyway. Riya and Ishaan were chatting casually over dinner and none seemed to mind that Natasha was not talking. She finished as fast as she could and left. She needed some time alone. Far away from the pollution of Delhi, the sky was clear and she could see the stars distinctly. The beauty of the star-spangled sky was lost on the lonely, grieving heart of a young girl in love. She could only think of what she could have done differently.

Why was her heart beating so hard? Why should it matter if Veer was with Amyra? They were married. They should be able to spend some time together. She knew that marriages were complicated and there were indiscretions that were forgotten, yet it was bothering her that they could be together. *Would they sleep together? Would he kiss Natasha like he kissed her? Would he?*

35

NATASHA HAD BEEN up till the wee hours of the morning to confirm if Veer was back. She kept on checking through her window. The road that led to Veer's cottage passed by her cottage. He could not go back without crossing her cottage. She was restless. She called up Nani in the middle of the night, and she woke up startled.

'Are you okay, beta?'

'Yes, Nani, I am okay. It's just that I am a little perplexed about a situation, so thought I would speak to you.'

Natasha told Nani nearly everything but replaced herself with her friend, and Veer and Amyra with two other names. Nani got a whiff of what was going on but she kept up with Natasha's story. She heard her out patiently.

'Nani, what do you think my friend should do?'

Nani took a long pause and replied, 'Beta, your friend is a very sweet girl. I wonder how I have never met her, considering I know most of your friends. Anyway, your friend should always remember that the most important thing in the whole world is one's self-respect. She should never do anything that demeans her. No matter who she loves, she must love herself more. She must always look for someone who values her and respects her for who she is. Even if there is a previous relationship, *he* must seek her out. Even if he has any baggage from a previous relationship, she must accept him only when he is a free man. There must be love, but respect takes precedence in a relationship, if you want it to last.'

Nani was feeling protective of Natasha and wanted to reach out to her and tell her to come back, to tell her that marriage was way more complicated than she could comprehend, but Natasha would have to figure it out on her own.

Natasha thanked Nani for being there. She knew that every word Nani had said was right, but she still didn't want to internalize it and act on it. She had once read that a woman should show more affection than she feels and not less, if she were to secure the man. However, as contrary as that was to Nani's advice, Natasha wanted to act on it. She made a promise to herself to tell Veer how she felt. She was planning how she would tell him when slumber caught up with her and she dozed off.

Natasha was jumping from one horse to the other, like a warrior. She was chasing Veer. She had been riding horses for a very long time and had crossed various rivers and mountains, with Veer leading her. Then she saw that Veer's horse took a big leap across a gorge, with an enormous, angry river flowing at the deep end. Natasha's horse stopped just short of jumping. Natasha could see Amyra waiting for Veer on the other side of the gorge. She welcomed him with open arms and kissed him, all the time looking at Natasha. She was challenging Natasha to take the jump. Natasha was trying very hard to make her horse jump but it wouldn't budge. Natasha looked on as a big, heart-shaped, red hot air balloon appeared from nowhere and both Veer and Amyra climbed into the wicker basket suspended underneath it. The balloon started rising from the ground. Amyra waved goodbye to her as it rose further. Natasha made one desperate attempt to jump across the gorge and this time, the horse did. She held on to its reins as it tried to finish the journey across the gorge in slow motion. She was so focused on the jump that she didn't notice that the hot air balloon was way beyond her reach now. When she looked up, she realized that the balloon was gone and at the same moment, the horse failed to reach the other side and started plunging into the gorge. Now, they were free-falling, though, somehow, she was still saddled in the horse. She fell in the furious river with a splash and woke up at the exact moment.

She was still on her bed, under the covers, neatly tucked in. She realized that she was dreaming all this while. She was happy that she didn't drown in the river, but she was sad that Veer had gone up in the hot air balloon with Amyra.

Was this dream God's way of telling her to let go? Or was it just her subconscious mind—her insecurity—acting up? She needed to get a grip on the situation. She couldn't keep going back and forth on her decision. Either she should follow her mind and let go of the idea of Veer, or she should pursue her heart's desire and make Veer hers. It had to be her decision and she needed to do it fast. But what about Veer? He had never clearly said what he wanted. He did say that he had been thinking about doing that for a long time before he had kissed her. Did it mean he loved her? Or did he just want to kiss her? She knew she loved him, but she wasn't sure of his feelings towards her. Amyra had complicated everything; she had ruined everything.

Natasha was determined not to let Amyra ruin things further for her. She was still wondering whether Veer had slept with Amyra, if he was back yet and if at all he wanted to speak to her, when she saw a notification for an unread message blinking on her phone. It was from Veer. Her heart was beating wildly. She leapt up on her bed and checked the time. It was noon. *She had slept through the whole morning and nobody had bothered to wake her up.* She clicked on the message. Veer had messaged, 'Care for a walk?' at 10 in the morning.

She felt a variety of emotions all at the same time. Happy. Sad. Angry. Frustrated. Everything together. *She was dreaming about horses and balloons while Veer was waiting for a reply from her. How frustrating is that?*

She groaned loudly and started typing a reply, 'Sorry, just saw your message. Shall we go now?' She had to make the effort after the faux pas. She didn't wait for the reply and started getting ready. A quick bath and a beautiful lavender wool dress with tights and some makeup were enough to make her look irresistible. Since the day looked sunny enough, she decided to let go off the long coat and opted for a wrap instead. She was putting on her boots when the arrival of a message on the phone was signalled by the beeping sound. It was Veer.

'Okay. Will meet you outside your cottage in five minutes.'

36

NATASHA'S HAIR WAS glistening in the sun. She looked magnificent in the lavender dress and big shades. She looked glamorous. Veer realized that he was seeing her like this for the first time since their dinner date in Landour. She looked at him and waved. Veer responded with another wave and joined her.

'So, where are we going?' Natasha looked like she was in a good mood.

'I had thought we would go for a walk, but now that I see you are dressed to kill,' he said flirtatiously, 'I have changed my plan. We will go for lunch instead.'

He took out his mobile and asked for the car to be brought to Natasha's cottage. Natasha liked the backhanded compliment. It made her feel like a woman. That he liked how she looked made her somehow feel confident. *As if she was seeking his approval. She was not. She was not that kind of a woman.* Yet, she had been feeling inadequate with Amyra around, and Veer's compliment and the way he looked at her made her feel beautiful.

He booked a table at the Urban Bistro. She had seen it while coming back from the adventure park. It was a cute little restaurant with an incredible view of the mountains. Incidentally, she had thought of visiting the cozy little place when she had passed by it the day before. Now that they were going there, she could only hope they served good food. Veer had kept the conversation very simple and general. They had talked about the cold weather, the mountains, the different colours of the sun and the dirty but happy children that they saw on the road. All she wanted to ask him was if he was with Amyra at night and what they did, but she waited patiently.

Unlike the last time they lunched together, this time Natasha knew what she wanted. She was very calm but she could see that Veer was nervous. He was fidgeting with his phone and his hair, and had ordered only a cup of coffee. Natasha was waiting for him to begin 'the talk', but he was stalling. So, she decided to ask him how his script was progressing.

'It's nearly finished, Natasha. I am writing the climax. A few more days of work and then I will be done.'

Veer was dressed in chinos and a hoodie. The combination of beige and black was very casual, comfortable, yet classic. The black of the hoodie was bringing out the black of his eyes.

'Do you mind if I order a drink?' he asked. Natasha nodded in approval. He called the waiter over, cancelled the coffee and ordered a single malt scotch on the rocks.

They were sitting in the corner of the bistro. There were book cabinets on both sides and Natasha felt at home. After a few sips of the drink and a slice of the thin-crust pizza, Veer looked in his element.

'Natasha, what would you say if you were asked to make a confession?' he asked, looking directly into her eyes from across the table. She was surprised with his question, but took up the challenge.

'I will answer this question only if you answer it first.' Natasha could see his eyes softening.

'I asked you first.' He took another sip and asked the waiter to repeat the drink, 'but I will answer the question after you.'

Natasha had finished the pizza and her coffee. She was feeling good, but for the butterflies in her stomach. She was trying to strike a balance between a politically correct reply and what she really wanted to confess. But she decided in favour of her heart and threw caution to the wind.

'Veer, if I had to confess, I would confess that I have feelings for you.'

She looked at her phone screen and not at Veer, because her heart was beating violently. She felt that if she looked into his eyes, he would know the depth of her feelings, and she wanted to keep it casual. She waited for him to respond.

He took a sip of his drink and said, 'Go on.'

She looked at him and said, 'I have had the hugest crush on you since I met you and even at the risk of making a fool of myself, I am confessing it to you, because it is too much to bear for me. I have never felt so drawn to anyone. I have tried to tell myself that I must focus on my career—I am a fairly career-driven person as you know—but somehow, my heart is singing a different tune. So here it is, I have confessed.'

Veer's face did not register any surprise. In fact, she could feel him relax a bit after hearing her. Natasha was feeling uncomfortable seeing his reaction—or rather, non-reaction.

Veer took his time. He had a lot to say. He had heard exactly what he was hoping she would say. It was a relief. He had fallen in love with her on the very first day when he had rescued her. Her beauty and her innocence were the least important of her traits. For such a young person, this girl was extremely focused and worked with precision. He was impressed with her insight on Guru Dutt's and Satyajit Ray's work. She paid attention to detail and was not scared to ask questions. She was probably the brightest girl he had met since Amyra. She would be a filmmaker to watch out for. It didn't matter though. He had lost his heart to her, even when he didn't know who she was. That first snowfall and how she had played with it, reminded him of the beautiful childhood he had had. He had forgotten how happy he had been as a child till her arrival in his life. He had so much to tell her that he did not know where to begin.

'Natasha, you know I am married to Amyra.'

Natasha winced. She was scared of what he was going to say next.

He reached across the table and put his hand on hers. The touch of his warm fingers calmed her down. 'Amyra and I got married five years back and dated two years before that. Effectively, we have been together for seven years of my thirty-two years of life. She was already an established model when I came to this industry. By doing my movies, she not only gave me credibility in front of the producers and audience, she also gave me the launch pad that not many are lucky enough to find. She is to me what Guru Dutt was to Waheeda Rehman.'

Natasha knew it then. He still loved her. She felt broken. It was beautiful that he could love a woman like that, but it was most unfortunate that the object of his affection was another woman. Her eyes were welling up, but he was still going on. She had to focus hard to hear what he was saying.

'Our marriage has fallen on bad times, not because we are bad people, but because we are passionate people fallen on bad times.

Amyra is here because she wants to give this marriage another try and I have been reasoning it out for the last few days as to what is the best that I can do. I was so drawn towards you that I was completely losing myself.'

Natasha felt her heart skip a beat. *Maybe there was hope.*

'When I kissed you for the first time, I couldn't believe the rush of emotions. I had never felt like that. I wanted more and more and so much more that I had to rush away.' Veer's hands were now holding Natasha's tightly. He was looking into her eyes and not looking away. 'Natasha, I wanted to make you mine. I had to tell myself that you are a young apprentice, probably out on your own for the first time, and interning for me; I can't take advantage of you. It would not be right, but every fibre in my body wanted you. When you got lost the other day, I felt as anxious as when the plane carrying my parents went missing. I kissed you that night with the motive to let you know that I loved you.' He was still looking at her.

She raised her eyes to look at him. She could see that he meant it. *He meant it. He loved her. Veer loved her.*

'You stopped me from going further and you were right to do so. I was angry at that moment but it was the best decision. I was thinking emotionally and you were thinking practically. The flight in the paraglider was one of the best moments of my life, Natasha. Seeing you conquer your fear and scale those heights was fantastic. If I had to confess, I would confess that I love you. That I have loved you ever since that rainy evening when I picked you up in my arms for the first time.' He was looking at her with so much love that tears sprung from her eyes.

She was happy that he loved her too, but she knew this was not it. There was more to it.

'Amyra has breast cancer,' he paused.

She was shocked to know that, he could see.

'She has been suffering alone. She is a brave girl but she is seeking me out now. I can't turn her away. I am not that man. I am still married to her and I feel responsible for her. At some level, I even love her. I guess I always will. She was there with me when I was nothing. She held me when I had lost everything; I had no hope and no career. I have to be there for her now. She looks very strong as if nothing can affect her, but she is really fragile right now. Last night when she told me, I couldn't believe this could happen to us. I mean, her career will be over once the treatment kicks in. She is scared of the chemotherapy and losing her hair and her breasts. She cried like a baby yesterday, Natasha. I am sure you understand what I am feeling for her. She was not only my wife, she was also my best friend. Friends can fight, but they also make up. She needs me and I am going to do the right thing by her. No matter what I feel for you, I owe her more.'

Natasha was not surprised at the depth of his emotions. He was an emotional man. She had fallen for a man who was a man of his word. A man who respected relationships. A man who would stand by a friend in distress. A man who would take care of a sick wife, even when they had been living separately and fighting for divorce for over a year. He was the type of man who knew how to love. The kind of love she wanted. The kind of love her parents had for each other. The kind of love that was written about in book and novels. Natasha had chosen well. But at the wrong time.

They walked back from the restaurant as friends, who didn't know what was destined. They knew that they loved each other but life had other plans. They had decided that Natasha will continue as his intern and will be an AD for his film when it goes on the floor.

Natasha had clarity, but she didn't feel content. Veer said he loved her, he had said the words she had wanted to hear—but there was no future with him. Even if he loved her, he couldn't be hers. She was not that kind of a woman. She knew that he was doing the right thing. She also knew it would be very stressful for her to work with him, but she wanted to be around him. So, she had made a decision to stay on and communicated the same to him. He also wanted her around. He was happy that she understood. With an agreement etched on their minds and love in their hearts, Natasha and Veer completed the walk back to the Eco Park and went their separate ways.

37

AMYRA WALKED UP to Natasha's cottage in the middle of the night. She had been meaning to talk to her for a while, but something had held her back. She zipped up her jacket as a draught of wind ruffled her hair and sent shivers down her spine. It was a particularly cold night. It looked like it would snow. The light from the lamp made the fog around it look like an orange cloud. She was reminded of the umpteen walks she had taken with Veer in the foggy weather. He loved the fog and would always drag her out. She resisted but secretly wished he would take her out so she could hug him and make him put his arm around her. The other night, after spending the whole day at Adventure Zone, Amyra realized that Veer's feelings for Natasha were not fleeting. She knew he had fallen for her. She couldn't take it. She had been in this fragile state for months now. She had tried to reach Veer many times, but he had not responded.

She had wanted to work on her relationship. Amyra had realized that she had thrown away Veer and her relationship with him, like a fool, for nothing more than ego. She had to make the amends and she would—she had decided. However, she had never factored in another woman. She had been so confident that Veer could never fall for anyone else that when she saw the obvious signs of Veer being in love with Natasha, she ignored them. But it could not be ignored anymore. She would have to confront Natasha and take charge of this situation or she would lose Veer.

The door to Natasha's room was ajar. She knocked twice on her door. When there was no response, she entered. Natasha was sprawled on the bed and had her headphones on. She was watching something on the laptop. She was so engrossed in it that she didn't even realize when Amyra had come inside. Amyra tapped on her shoulder. She got up with a start.

'Hey, Amyra, please have a seat.' Natasha moved the blankets a little, creating some space on the bed.

Amyra looked ethereal. She was so delicate and feminine. Perfect skin and perfect facial features engulfed by a mass of perfect hair. Natasha could never be so beautiful. *Could anyone be so beautiful?* Natasha could not believe Amyra was dealing with a deadly disease like cancer.

'Natasha, I have come to talk to you about Veer.' Amyra didn't have the patience to be politically correct. She just went straight to the point, 'You know we are married, right?'

It was not a question. Natasha knew it was a statement and she could make out Amyra's militant tone. She didn't like where this was going. She had promised Veer that she would never let Amyra know that she knew about her disease. She patiently nodded.

'So, Natasha, we have been living separately for a while now as you must have read in the newspapers and magazines.' Amyra nervously ran a hand through her glossy shining hair. Natasha nodded in agreement. 'Love is a complicated thing and marriage is more complicated. You are too young to understand what actually happens in a marriage; how two people come together and make a whole. We have had our differences, we have said things to each other that were hurtful, but we never meant them. Both Veer and I are very passionate people and we believe that all is fair in love and war. A year away from him has made me realize what he means to me. It made me realize what my relationship meant to me, how much I value him and his friendship. I was lost in the glamorous world when he found me, Natasha. I had everything a young girl could dream of—an awesome career, a big house and lots of endorsements—yet, I was unhappy. I didn't have a family or a loved one to share it with. Veer gave me love; he gave me a family, a home. I felt complete when I was with him. And then something snapped between the two of us and it all went haywire. Maybe the evil eye,' she said with a smile. 'We went our separate ways, but we are joined at the hip, Natasha. We are one and the same. He loves me. I know. I am in love with him, Natasha, and will go to any lengths to secure his love.'

Natasha saw the determination on her face and realized that her heart was beating fast. She kept mum and Amyra continued.

'In the past few days, I have seen how Veer reacts when you are around. I know that he likes you. I know that you like him. I know that you feel there is more to it, but there isn't. It's just that. Infatuation. You are young; you will find someone else. He is a married man and he is out of bounds for you.'

Amyra was getting aggressive. Natasha felt guilty. She knew Amyra was correct. She had the moral high ground. Veer was married and he should be out of bounds, but she fell in love with him and he reciprocated. She would have retaliated and said a lot many things had she not known of Amyra's condition and Veer's decision. No matter what she said, the fact that Veer was going to stay with Amyra wouldn't change. She caved in and decided not to argue.

Amyra had stood up and was now standing at a distance from the bed, towering over Natasha.

'Natasha, you have to go. You have to go out of our lives. I want you to tell me what it is that you want in return so I can feel at peace.' Amyra sat down in a chair near the bed.

Natasha had not expected this. She had thought Amyra would be angry at her, scream at her or even ask her to stay away but to let go completely was something she had not deliberated upon. She had focused all her energies on surviving in the same vicinity as Veer; knowing that he loves her and that he can never be hers.

She never thought of going away. *She could. That would be the easy way out. What about her career?* She had not lost sight of why she had come to Mussoorie in the first place. Matters of the heart could not take precedence over matters of the mind. She had to endure being with Veer and all the heartache that would come with it, for her career. *Was it worth it?* Amyra was asking her to go away. She could go away. *Should she? Would it even matter to anyone if she went away? It would to Amyra. She wanted her out.* From her body language, Natasha could feel that she was not used to asking people for things. Natasha had nothing to look forward to as far as her relationship with Veer was concerned. All she could hope for was a few moments here and there. The practical student in her was still harping on about the great career opportunity that this would have been, but the girl in her, who was all heart, just wanted to get away. More opportunities would come her way. She was sure.

'Okay, Amyra, I will go away,' said Natasha, with as much

conviction as she could muster. She was fighting back tears, but told herself to get a grip and be strong.

Amyra relaxed a bit. 'Don't tell Veer I asked you to leave. He would not like it. Please let us have a fair chance at our marriage. That's my last request to you.' Amyra was overwhelmed.

With all the planning and the conniving and the constant fear of losing Veer, Amyra felt like she was losing it. She had kept her wits together with a lot of effort and she was emotionally drained. She rushed out of Natasha's room, without another word, tears streaming down her face.

Natasha flopped back on the bed and cried her heart out. When the tears dried up and there was only a vacuum left in her heart, she started packing. She called a cab company and booked a cab till Dehradun. As the cab pulled in, she was thinking of what she would say to Veer, but could not decide on it. She tugged at the loose ends of her heart and her jacket, to pull them together, and left. As the sun was climbing up the mountains, peeking out from the nooks and corners, somewhere near Dehradun, between delirium and nausea, she messaged Veer.

'I have to go. All this is too much for me. I hope you will understand.'

38

IT WAS RAINING cats and dogs in New Delhi. The beginning of the monsoon was always such a happy time, but not that day. Natasha had to catch the morning flight to Mumbai and the rain was messing up her plan. She walked in from Gate 1 at Terminal 3 of the Indira Gandhi International Airport. She was dressed in her trademark clothes—a pair of vegetable-dyed linen pants and a cotton kurta. Her perfect hair was hanging loosely, swept away from her face with the help of her D&G glasses. Smokey eyes and a black bindi were her USP. Big, oxidized silver earrings and a long silver chain with a traditional soorma box as a pendant adorned her. Kolhapuri chappals looked gorgeous on the manicured feet. Natasha loved toe rings and wore them on both her feet. She also wore a silver anklet that made a sweet sound when she walked. A huge Prada tote bag housed all her essentials and she was lugging around an overnighter for her stay at Mumbai.

Natasha was travelling to Mumbai for the film festival. She had been going there regularly for the past five years. In her late twenties now, Natasha was a well-travelled, more confident, cosmopolitan girl with a vast amount of experience. She had carved a niche for herself in the Mumbai film industry. For the first few years after leaving Veer in Dehradun, she interned with various filmmakers and worked as an AD with them. Later, she wrote a script for a short film and directed it with young actors. It was the story of a young tribal girl, who struggles with dyslexia and overcomes her handicap to succeed in life. It was sent as India's entry at the Oscars and was screened at the Cannes Film Festival too. She got a lot of recognition and people wanted to work with her. This year would mark the release of her first major feature film and the trailer of the movie was to be launched at the Mumbai Film Festival. It was her labour of love.

Natasha checked in at the Air India counter and went through the security, smiling at everyone. She was a happy person and she frequented the morning flight, so most of the Central Industrial Security Force staff on the morning shift recognized her. Suddenly, a lady with a sweet voice announced that the departure of the Air India flight to Mumbai had been delayed by three hours due to heavy rains. Natasha groaned. She hated it when flights got delayed. She had meticulously planned every hour of the day. Now, she would have to kill three hours at the airport. She thanked God that she was carrying her laptop. Once through with the security check, she went to the lounge and ordered a coffee.

As she was settling down in a sofa in the corner, she happened to glance diagonally across at the other corner. Her heart skipped a beat. It was Veer. She was just wondering whether to approach him or not when he looked up. Their eyes locked. And before she knew it, Veer had stood up and was walking up to her.

'What a happy coincidence this is! Natasha! How have you been?'

He came forward to hug her—a warm bear hug, like old friends. His hair was greying. He was in his mid-thirties and wore his age well. His hair still flopped to one side, but now he wore reading glasses. He was still the same handsome, sexy, six-foot-plus charmer and Natasha still loved him. In his signature beige and black, he looked a class apart.

'I am well,' Natasha replied with great difficulty.

She had practiced so many times what she would say to Veer if she happened to meet him, but words still failed her. He sat down across her.

'How have you been, Veer?'

'We will talk about me later; first tell me about yourself. It's been—what—five years since we have seen each other?' he said, looking at her. She confirmed. 'Five years, Natasha! How have you been?'

Natasha had been well. Not a day had gone by without her thinking of Veer. That day when she had left Dhanaulti, her heart had been broken. Veer had responded to her parting message with a few frantic calls, which she didn't take. She didn't have the strength.

She messaged him back: 'It's for the best, Veer. Please let me go. It's too hard for me to be around you.'

He had backed off, and hadn't called her after that.

Yayu, her best friend, had held her when she had cried over Veer, took her for movies and plays when she felt depressed and tried to cheer her up when she talked about the lost opportunity in terms of her career. Natasha carried on in life with the support of Yayu.

Her luck turned when Gazaffar called up and asked for her to assist him in a movie that he was making. He said that he was making up for the soup that he had landed her in. She had jumped at the opportunity. The movie was mostly shot in Australia and

New Zealand. Nani had taken a sabbatical and accompanied her to the faraway lands. She had kept herself absolutely occupied with work and disconnected from the online world.

A year passed. Gazaffar's film was ready to be released. Natasha had come to know of Amyra's career in Hollywood through various newspapers and had admired Veer's compassion and commitment. She had never contacted them though, and neither had they. One day, a picture of Amyra was leaked on the net. She was sitting on the lap of a handsome hunk, who was definitely not Veer. She was wearing couture as usual and looked fabulous. She didn't even look sick. She continued reading that article only to find out that Veer had divorced her a year back. *A year back!* The whole year, when she had been trying to run away from the whole world and had completely weaned herself away from the news and the Internet, Veer might have been trying to reach her. It was too late then. She had thought of reaching out to him, but more than a year had passed and they had not connected at all; she couldn't just call him. *What if he didn't feel the same way any more?*

Veer had settled abroad after his divorce from Amyra, taking up a teaching position at one of the film institutes in England. Natasha had got busy with her assignments and even though she always felt the urge to reach out to him, to reconnect and see what was left of those feelings that they had confessed to on that balmy day in Dhanaulti, time and distance complicated matters. Then there were speculations about Veer's love life and a new girl was in the picture every month. They were either snapped at a party or at a restaurant. All that put Natasha off. Even when she travelled to London for a shoot, she made sure they were never in the proximity. Veer also never reached out to her. He never wrote; he never messaged. He never tried to reconnect. Natasha was suddenly angry that he had never contacted her.

She looked at him and replied tersely, 'I have been alright, Veer. It's been a long journey. I am doing well professionally.'

'Yes, yes, I know about you. I have read about your professional rise. In fact, I have been following it very keenly. I am proud of what you have achieved. I watched your short film. It was exceptional. I could see you in every aspect of the film,' he said with such affection, that Natasha felt bad that she was so terse with him.

The waiter chose that very moment to bring her coffee. She needed a moment to gather herself. Natasha was feeling very emotional and she couldn't let him see that. In the last five years, she had not been able to be in a relationship with anyone, because of her feelings for him—feelings that never went away; never even faded. She was looking for him in every man she had dated. She was looking for the same passion that his kiss had incited in her, but that had never happened. She kept looking for that warm liquid feeling in her heart, which arose so quickly when he was around, even today, but it had never happened with anyone else. She always came back feeling restless and depressed after a date. And that he was snapped, happy and smiling, with these girls, didn't help her case. She needed to know what had been happening in his life.

'Veer, tell me about yourself. What have you been up to?'

'I am sure you know about my divorce from Amyra,' he said, looking at her. 'What you don't know is that Amyra had lied to me. She had lied to me about her cancer. She wasn't dying. She had tricked me. She had planned everything so meticulously that I could not see through her fraud till we went to Switzerland. Even in Mumbai, she had planned an elaborate visit to the doctor and even faked the MRIs and CT scans. She had paid the doctor to lie to me about her cancer. When we landed in Switzerland on the pretext of her treatment, she took me to a spa and said that the waters will calm her down. She was still her bubbly self, with no trace of an illness. That got me thinking and I started investigating. She was very particular about handling her medicines by herself. Once when she was out, I checked her medicines. All of them were vitamin and calcium tablets. When I confronted her, she confessed and said that she faked her illness because she didn't want to lose me.'

Natasha was shell-shocked to hear all this. She tried to say something but no words would come out from her mouth. She was furious. She, too, had been fooled. Cheated.

She should have trusted her instincts when she felt that Amyra was untrustworthy. She should have never believed her. What a perfect crime! Amyra had stolen what could have been some of the most beautiful moments of Natasha's life.

She was so lost in her thoughts that she had forgotten that Veer was still talking.

'... Dadi egged me to travel the world, and I did. I kept looking for inner peace in every nook and corner of the world and finally found it embedded deep within me.'

He ran a hand through his hair and adjusted his spectacles on the bridge of his nose. Natasha wanted to comfort him and hug him, but she held back.

'When I came to London, an offer to teach at the London Film Institute was lying in my inbox and I took it up. Since then, I have been teaching there. So, there it is—the last five years of my life in a nutshell. Nothing exciting, right?'

He winked at her and just like that, she was back to being a young girl, in love with the swashbuckling filmmaker. Something came over her and she asked what she was dying to know.

'Did you miss me even once during the last five years?'

Veer looked at her and said, 'Should I tell the truth or lie about it?' very sincerely.

'Lie about it,' Natasha replied sombrely.

'I didn't miss you at all. I didn't miss you every time it snowed. I didn't miss you every morning I woke up. I didn't miss you every night I went to sleep. I didn't miss you every time Dadi called from Mussoorie. I didn't miss you every time Amyra apologized for taking me away from you. I didn't miss you every time Amyra begged me to call you so she could apologize to you. I didn't even miss you when I divorced Amyra, and all I could think of was running back to you and seeking solace. I didn't miss you in every nook and corner of the world, seeking peace, when all I really wanted was to be back in India with you. I have not missed you even once in the last five years,' he finished, with tears in his eyes.

She heard him. He was not saying what she really wanted to hear.

'Why didn't you contact me after the divorce?' Natasha asked, holding back her tears.

Veer looked uncomfortable. He looked around for an ashtray and lit up a cigarette.

'Natasha, after you left from Dhanaulti that day, I knew something must have happened to have changed your mind. I mean, we had decided that you will continue working with me and then, all of a sudden, you packed your bags and left. Even when I tried calling you, you didn't take my call. I went directly to Amyra's room to confront her. I was very angry. When I reached Amyra's room, I saw her lying on the floor, unconscious. I spoke to her oncologist—who I later found out was already hand-in-glove with Amyra about her condition—on the phone in Mumbai. He told me that it would be best if I bring her to Mumbai ASAP. I did as I was asked. Amyra was rushed to Mumbai in an air ambulance. Her treatment had to begin immediately in Switzerland. The doctor had not given her much time.' He lit up another cigarette and continued to look away at the planes on the tarmac.

'To keep all this a secret, we had to tell the media that Amyra and I were getting back together and going for our second honeymoon. After a lot of speculation, the media finally left us alone. We reached Switzerland. As I told you, she had planned everything meticulously. Once I got to know about her drama, I asked her about her conversation with you. She told me that she had asked you to go away. She was apologetic and had asked me to leave her be and go back to India to you. To tell you the truth, I had felt very angry at that moment and really wanted to come back. I rushed out, walked in to a local tavern and drank till I passed out. When I woke up, I found Amyra sitting next to me. She still insisted that she loved me and had done everything for the sake of our marriage. I was fed up of all her lies and shenanigans. I had lost you; I had also lost any love or respect I had for Amyra.'

He looked at Natasha.

'By the end of all the drama with Amyra, I had changed as a person. The fact that I was duped by my wife, and lost the girl I had loved wholeheartedly, changed the way I looked at life. I read about your progress on various film news websites and got to know about you through some friends in the industry. I wanted to reach out to you, but I didn't think it was right. You were doing so well professionally and I didn't want to confuse you or complicate your life. It would have been a selfish thing to do. Therefore, I held back and looked after my other responsibilities, including Dadi and my business. I also took up the teaching post. It's been more than two years since, but I haven't made a movie yet. I have been running away from that part of myself. The director in me has taken a back seat since my heart broke. I never told you,' he reached out and held her hand, 'after our first kiss, I had left a book for you and dog-eared the page that I had wanted you to read. I had wanted you to know how much that had meant to me. Your innocence and your passion had reminded me of all that I could have been and all that I wanted to be—most of all, a better man.'

With tears streaming down from her eyes, Natasha stood up and went closer to him. He got up in response and welcomed her in his arms. She cried her heart out, oblivious to the surroundings and to the numerous passengers staring at them. He kissed her head, and caressed her head and back, trying to calm her down, while struggling hard to hold himself back. Natasha looked up at him and he reached down to kiss her—a life-giving kiss that had the power to move the heavens and the earth; a kiss that went from sweet to passionate to intense in a split second.

Veer ended the kiss, kissed her forehead and said, 'Let's get out of here,' with desire in his eyes.

Natasha held back, 'Say you love me.'

Veer laughed and said, 'Of course I love you, my dearest. I never knew I was capable of loving quite as much. I love you like crazy. You remember how, at the end of *Kaagaz Ke Phool*, Guru Dutt and Waheeda meet in that song, '*Waqt ne kiya kya haseen sitam*'? That's exactly what is happening to us. The difference is that we get to have our happy ending, my darling. I will make sure we do.'

Natasha kissed him in return and ended it before they completely lost it. She threw some money on the table and collected her bags. They ran out of the airport like two happy children, laughing and giggling, looking forward to a beautiful future.

Natasha looked out of the window of a car that they had gotten into. As it navigated the morning rush hour traffic, dark clouds were giving way to a beaming sun. She looked at Veer and thought, *she was where she always belonged, cradled in his arms, breathing the same air that he breathed*. She kissed his cheek, put her head on his shoulder and closed her eyes. Life had come full circle.